Wake of the Huntress

Amanda Tullis

CONTENTS

For Grandma Kieko and Grandpa Glenn, who were always ready and happy to indulge my childhood love of stories and imagination. God brings us the people who are meant to be in our lives, and I feel beyond blessed that he brought you into mine. Kieko, I hope you enjoy my story, and Glenn, how I wish you could be here to read it. Thank you both for your lifelong love and support. There are simply no words to describe how much you mean to me.

PROLOGUE

"Dormastis ruled, but now he sleeps. Forever in darkness, but never in peace."

-Ancient poem, author unknown

Darkness is cold, heavy, and penetrating. Darkness is universal. Some embrace it. Some run from it. Some avoid it at all costs. Being afraid of the dark does not mean one is afraid of the darkness itself but of what might be *in* it. Darkness makes one very aware of oneself and the possibility of what might be around them. It has a habit of working its way into the flesh, the bones, and the soul.

This was the feeling that engulfed the woman who stood at the top of the old dungeon stairway, her trembling fingers gripping the door frame with one hand. There would typically be torches lighting the hall and the way down the staircase, perhaps even a guard at the entrance. This dungeon, however, was long abandoned. The only sound to be heard was the occasional drip of water falling from the grimy ceiling.

The woman glanced around to ensure she hadn't been followed and jumped slightly as the courtyard clock struck midnight. She froze for a moment after the last gong, thankful those who lived in the castle with her had learned to sleep through the hourly disturbance. She could not afford to be caught. This crumbling old corner of the fortress was not often visited by anyone, let alone a member of the royal family. Its purpose was long forgotten, and no one cared enough to have it repaired. So here this old hall sat, the perfect setting for the nefarious deeds that now took place in the rotting chambers below.

Content that she was alone, the woman turned back to the blackness and shuddered in the draftiness coming from the empty doorway. *Get ahold of yourself, Marania,* she thought. *Facing this is nothing compared to what you've just done.* She took a deep breath and started down the stairs, gingerly closing the creaking wooden door behind her. The rancid air stung her nose, and the stone wall under her fingertips felt wet and rough. She wished she had a light, but it had been forbidden. She would have to feel her way down.

The duchess had never been in darkness such as this. It was almost suffocating. She felt herself begin to sweat, although she suspected that if the room had been lighter, she would have been able to see her breath in the cold. She made her way down the staircase one step at a time. With every step, she reached forward with her foot as far as she dared and finally found the floor flat. She must have reached the hallway between the old cells. When the Scythe of Dormastis first approached her, they seemed so powerful and elegant, the perfect group of people to help her. She wasn't sure what she'd been expecting for her first meeting with them, but it certainly wasn't this.

At the end of the hallway, she could just barely make out the glow from a small, sputtering candle in the wall. According to the map she'd memorized and burned, that was her destination. Her sweaty hand shook, and she tightened her grasp on the tiny vial she held, the liquid inside still warm. With a deep breath, she started forward again, feeling her heart pound and chest tighten with every step.

As she approached the glow of the candlelight, Marania couldn't tell if she was shivering from cold, fear, or the sheer adrenaline of what she had just done. Murder wasn't something she was prone to. At least, that's what she'd thought until tonight. She was dreading what might happen in the morning when her act was discovered. No one would know it had been her. She'd made sure of that. It was the first terrifying yet necessary step toward getting what she deserved. Now, she had only to present the proof of her loyalty to those who could get her there.

Having reached the candle, she carefully felt along the ledge it was resting on, willing her fingers to find what her eyes could not see. *There!* A tiny notch in the stones, engraved with the shape of a scythe. She pushed, and the stone reluctantly gave way with a scraping sound, triggering the hidden door to slowly creak open and reveal another hallway. This one was lit on both sides with torches, and Marania had to shield her eyes from the burst of light. When she moved her hand away from her face, she gasped and took a step back, finding a man in a black robe standing before her. A hood covered his head, and his face was masked in silver. She'd been warned her escort would be in disguise.

"Lady Marania, we've been expecting you. Please follow me." He turned and walked down the hall.

Marania took a moment to steel herself, then followed. It was a small comfort that she recognized her companion's voice. *It's only Lord Kels. You sat next to him at supper this evening and discussed the gardens.* She hadn't expected the proceedings to be so mysterious and formal, although their supposed connection to Dormastis should have been indicative of some of their...customs. As far as she was aware, the ancient sorcerer was nothing more than a myth. On the other hand, even in the legends, he wasn't exactly what one would call benevolent.

Following Lord Kels down the sparsely lit hallway, she began to hear muffled voices, which grew more distinct as they approached what must have once been an oversized communal cell. The floor was peppered with dripping candles, stuck to the stones with the melting wax, casting an eerie glow on the walls. In the middle of the chamber, the assembled company of The Scythe of Dormastis circled around another engraving of their namesake tool, surrounded by delicately carved flames. Surprisingly, there were only six figures, all wearing the same dark hoods and chanting in an ancient and forgotten language, their voices low and unsettling.

As they approached the circle of figures, Kels motioned for Marania to pause behind him. The chanting died down, then abruptly stopped, leaving the room in a deafening silence. The two nearest members had left enough of an opening for Kels to lead her into the middle of the circle. She glanced nervously. Though every man or woman under those dark hoods and silver masks was a member of the royal court, they had all betrayed their ruler with one common goal in mind—to put the duchess on the throne.

Once in the center of the company, Kels stepped aside. Marania was left staring as another man approached. His crimson robe and gold mask singled him out from the others, and his slow, rigid movements seemed to obscure the rest of the imposing scene from her vision. She fought the urge to back away and yet couldn't even make herself blink. Attempting to smother her fear, she straightened her back and drew herself up to her full height.

"Lady Marania Donavar," the man greeted her in a honeyed, thin voice. "I was beginning to worry you wouldn't make it to our little gathering. We are pleased to have you join us for the first time."

She tried to keep her voice steady. "Thank you for having me, My Lord." *Do I know this one?* His voice wasn't familiar, and she didn't dare ask for a name. *Does it really matter?* No. It didn't.

"Do you have what we requested?" The man extended his hand expectantly. Marania looked at the tiny vial she held that contained the blood. Her sister's blood. She gingerly placed it in his waiting palm, and the man examined its contents. "It's hers?"

Marani felt a shiver go down her spine at the fresh memory of entering her sister's chambers with a dagger in her gloved hand. Not even an hour had passed since. "Yes. I took care of it myself."

A wave of murmurs rounded the assembly. Her host cocked his head. "Very daring of you, I must say. You're sure it's *completely* taken care of?" He sounded as if he was testing her.

"Without a doubt."

"And the weapon?"

"Disposed of. Furthermore, no one will ever know it was me." This man didn't need to know "disposed of" simply meant keeping it on her person from now on.

Satisfied, the man turned away from her to address the circle. "My friends, the future queen has completed the first stage of our plan. We shall now proceed."

He removed the cork stopper from the vial and slowly poured the blood into the engraving on the floor, speaking the same old language from the chants as he did so. Marania watched as it flowed into the grooves. The image now looked stained and grotesque, much like the blade she still had concealed under her skirts. Once the vial was empty, the man gestured for the group to join the chant. The unsettling chorus of voices returned, giving Marania a shudder as they filled her ears. Her eyes widened as the blood on the floor slowly evaporated and disappeared. She had never seen magic with her own two eyes.

The voices stopped abruptly.

"Dormastis has accepted our offering and will help us in our endeavor," their leader stated with finality.

Marania frowned. "Isn't Dormastis a myth? And even if he isn't, what does he have to do with me taking over the throne?"

A sneer entered the man's voice. "Is that what you've been taught? That magic does not exist?"

What she'd been taught was that Dormastis did not exist. At the moment, however, she didn't see that fact helping her. "Magic itself is rare enough," she stated carefully. "On that basis alone, someone as powerful as he is said to have been is impossible."

The man's eyes glinted through his mask. Marania thought she could see even his terrifying smile under the painted mouth. His face came within inches of hers, and she took a step back.

"You do not know how wrong you are, my dear. While Dormastis no longer exists in this realm, his power is everything you have heard and more. We are his acolytes here, and we, with the help of his magic, will succeed in our plan." The man backed up and crossed his arms over his chest.

Marania had not been aware of any magic involved in securing her place on the throne. Nearly a thousand years had passed since the last of Enderhail's magic had all but disappeared. "If Dormastis is real, and he has this power, why now? And why help me?"

"The world is poised for change. He believes you are best suited to help guide Enderhail through that change. You possess the kind of strength and conviction that will be required for such a period."

The duchess was slightly taken aback. It all sounded too good to be true. But if this sorcerer was indeed what he was purported to be, why not her? After all, the throne was meant to be hers. She committed murder to prove it. It wouldn't be in vain. "Thank him for me. For trusting me with the task."

"Thank *you* for being willing to prove your loyalty. The wheels have now been set in motion, but things cannot proceed too quickly. We must bide our time if we don't want to arouse suspicion. We will approach you when the next stage of the plan is ready." He bent to break a candle off the floor and handed it to her.

Marania nodded respectfully, acknowledging her dismissal, and turned to go back the way she had come.

"Oh, and one more thing," her host caught her off guard, "you know, there is still one small...barrier that may keep us from achieving our goal. Are you familiar with the race of nomadic people known as the Havani?"

"Of course I am," Marania said flatly. "My sister's husband hates them. He doesn't believe they can be trusted."

"Well, he may be right in that, my lady. The Havani are a race who possess the power of Sight, the ability to catch glimpses of the future. They can even See past and present if they are strong enough. They don't all have this ability, but enough do..." He hesitated, his air of control faltering slightly for the first time. "It's entirely possible that one of these Havani might have Seen us enacting our plan and will take action to stop it."

Marania scoffed. "Why would they possibly interfere? They don't even acknowledge my brother-in-law as their king. Nor did they acknowledge my father, who foolishly accepted their self-proclaimed right to autonomy. They still have no respect for the crown."

"That may be the case, but it wouldn't necessarily keep them from reporting what they See in vision if they perceived it to be the right thing to do. They may not submit to the monarchy, but they consider themselves to be honorable." The Scythe leader swallowed a laugh of contempt. "Do you think you could somehow…persuade the king to, shall we say, take care of them? At least the Seers, that is. That task will also serve to distract him from discovering our plot."

The duchess calmed herself. "I'm sure I can do that," she replied. "There can't be many of them, and there must be a way to differentiate between who has this power and who does not."

"I'm sure. Now, you know who you can trust. Speak of this to no one else." The man put one finger to where his mouth would be.

Marania nodded and finally left the room, her footsteps quickening as she disappeared down the hall.

The crimson-cloaked man stared after her and narrowed his coal-black eyes under his mask. Until this evening, he hadn't been wholly convinced she would do what had been asked. He wasn't often surprised, but Marania had fulfilled her end of the bargain. The queen had died at the hands of her own sister. Now, she just had to do what she was told and leave the rest to him.

The deep voice of Lord Kels interrupted his thoughts. "I didn't realize it would be so easy to make her turn on her sister. How did you manage it, Talis?"

"When one wants something badly enough, they will sacrifice almost anything to get it. I know from experience." Talis turned to Kels. "She will only talk to you and Lady Enid. Try to keep her focused. The rest of us will work to expand our number and influence. We're going to need all the help we can get."

"What if she discovers our real plan?" Kels asked.

Talis looked around at the few other members of the group, who were removing their masks and robes. "By the time that happens, it will be far too late. Those vagabonds need to be gone before our master can regain his power. If we can get that pathetic king to do the dirty work for us, no one will be the wiser." An evil smile played at the corners of the golden mouth on his mask. "And if he happens to die in the process, all the better."

CHAPTER ONE

"Do not let any kind of beauty deceive you. There's no telling what might be hiding beneath the surface."

-Havani proverb

Lady Marania stared up at the imposing towers of Castle Felhold, its torches casting dancing shadows down the outer walls. She smiled to herself, her lips turning up into a satisfied sneer. This cold autumn night was to be the beginning of the end. Soon, they would all be gone, tragically taken from this world too early. Grief-stricken, she would reluctantly take up the mantle left behind by her family and restore the House of Donavar. Enderhail would have its first sovereign queen. A ruler it deserved. She'd spent her whole life formulating her plans to strengthen the crown and better the kingdom. Her first official act would be to return her home to its rightful name, Castle Donavar. Then she would–

She turned sharply at the sound of a twig cracking behind her. As she peered into the gloom, a shadow emerged from the trees. The cloaked Havani woman hobbled toward the duchess, leaning heavily on her walking stick. Marania removed her hood as the old woman came up beside her. "Zepatra." She gave her companion a respectful nod.

Zepatra pulled down her own hood and kept her gaze on the castle on the hill above them. "Looks can be deceiving, can't they, Lady Marania? The castle is so regal and beautiful on the outside, yet we all know something ugly and wicked is happening within its walls." Her voice rasped as she spoke and turned to face the younger woman.

Marania didn't like the way Zepatra was looking at her. "What do you mean?" she asked nervously. Was this village fortune teller really one of the fabled Seers of the nomadic Havani people? Did she know what she had done?

"Your sister, the queen, was killed only a year ago. Let's not pretend the poor serving boy they arrested is really guilty. He wouldn't even have had access to the queen's chambers."

Marania tensed, reaching for the small blade concealed under her cloak. She knew it was a mistake to bring in an outsider! She should have just put on a disguise and done this part herself. They would have to push the plan back a few days so she could prepare. It would be inconvenient...but one more body wouldn't hurt...

Zepatra had turned her eyes back to the castle. "Mark my words, there's something sinister going on behind those walls. One day, they won't be able to contain it anymore. Then we'll all be in trouble."

Marania felt her stomach turn over, but she relaxed slightly as Zepatra addressed her again.

"Do you have what we agreed upon, my dear?" The Havani woman was stoic as she asked the question.

Marania slowly reached for a pouch at her waist. "500 gold pieces," she confirmed as she tossed it to the old woman.

Zepatra caught it with surprising agility and weighed it in her gnarled hand. "Everything appears to be in order." She nodded with satisfaction as she drew the pouch into the folds of her cloak. "The king will no longer be able to ignore his hatred of us." A gravelly chuckle escaped from her throat. "I'll make sure of that."

The duchess still couldn't believe how easy it had been to convince the old bat to do what she asked: come to the castle and tell the king of a false vision to exploit his mistrust of the Havani people and their powers, to make him finally turn on them for good. When she sought Zepatra out a few days before, she half expected to be turned out of her shop with a furious outburst of the native Havani language, perhaps even threatened to be blackmailed with the information she divulged. Instead, the fortune teller listened thoughtfully to her request, then negotiated her price as only a good tradeswoman would. Marania recalled sitting in the cottage with her mouth hanging open in shock. She'd heard that Zepatra wasn't on the best terms with her people, but she hadn't expected her to be so open and callous about it.

Her spoils safely hidden away, Zepatra locked eyes with Marania for a few moments. The Havani was still as stone, making the younger woman feel very exposed. She shifted uncomfortably, studying Zepatra in the faint glow of the castle torchlight. The fortune teller was old, thin, and bent with age. Her long, frizzy hair was mostly gray, and her skin was wrinkled and sagging. But underneath the years, Marania caught the remaining recognizable traits of the Havani race: raven black hair, alabaster skin, and bright blue eyes. Zepatra must have been a striking woman when she was younger. The Havani had a rather magnetic effect on those around them. Perhaps this was one of the reasons the king disliked them so much. He didn't approve of anything he couldn't immediately understand.

Marania shook her head in bewilderment. "I must admit, Zepatra, I'm still rather surprised at your willingness to subject your own people to this kind of potential harm."

Zepatra gave her a sly smile. "I am old, dear. Older than you might imagine, in fact. I left my tribe when I was young because I preferred the idea of village life over roaming the land in wagons and scavenging for food. In reality, there are quite a few village-dwelling Havani in this kingdom. Though it's not the life most would prefer. We exist throughout all the kingdoms of Terravalia. There aren't many tribes who follow the old ways like those in Enderhail." Her gaze drifted briefly as if she was watching the past play out before her. "I love my people. But in their eyes, I betrayed them long ago." She sighed. "The world is about to change. The last time this happened, the Havani were unwilling to adapt. That cannot be allowed to happen again."

What does that mean? Marania felt her stomach turn over with anxiety once again. The older woman clearly wasn't being completely honest about her willingness to accept the terms of their deal. Should she press the issue? Demand to know why Zepatra was so prepared to do as she asked?

The Havani woman caught Marania's quizzical stare and glowered a warning.

Suddenly fearful of the silence and her guest, the duchess quickly brought up another subject. "Are you afraid of what may happen after tonight?"

Zepatra shook her head, apathy returning to her face. "I plan on leaving the kingdom as soon as I complete the task you've given me. It will likely no longer be safe for any Havani after tonight."

Marania nodded. Their primary target was the Seers, but it was entirely possible that all the nomads would be at some level of risk. They had no idea exactly how the king would react. "If that is the case, run west to the border pass. I will keep you from being pursued." She turned to leave. "Wait fifteen minutes after I have left and then approach the front gate. Tell the guard you have an urgent message for the royal family. Don't take no for an answer. The guard will likely fetch the king's chief advisor to question you. Do what you must to convince him. If you absolutely cannot get him to let you in, take your gold and go. I will come up with another plan." She furrowed her brow. "Are you truly one of the Seers, Zepatra?"

"Does it matter?" the woman asked matter of factly.

"No, I suppose it doesn't," Marania conceded. She'd find out how to tell them apart on her own.

"Do you ever fear for your own life, my dear? After what happened to your sister?"

Marania turned her back to the Havani woman and started to walk away. "I believe we all get what's coming to us in the end. Whether we like it or not." She walked away, feeling Zepatra's eyes boring into her.

Marania hiked up the small hill to the castle gate, her heart thundering as she approached the guards. Oldart, the captain of the guard, was on duty, and he waved her through.

"Did you enjoy your evening walk, Duchess?" He gave a slight bow.

"Yes, thank you, Oldart. It was very...enlightening," she said casually.

Oldart raised an eyebrow but said nothing. Marania knew they all thought she'd been acting strangely recently. The castle's inhabitants assumed her odd behavior was nothing more than the grief of a loving sister. If only they knew the truth.

Once inside, the duchess made her way up the stairs to the great hall, where the king was sitting with a few members of his court, poring over some important and likely complex governing documents. She relished the thought of that being her job one day, having the power to decide the fate of the kingdom and how it was run, a council whose sole purpose was to help enumerate and enforce her will. The future Queen Marania wouldn't be afraid to assert dominance over her people and the neighboring kingdoms, unlike her late father and the current monarch.

King Steflan Felhold glanced up at his sister-in-law as she took a seat at the table but didn't acknowledge her otherwise. They had never been overly fond of one another but managed to be civil, for the most part. It had been that way since he'd first arrived from the nearby kingdom of Dalheim to prepare to marry Alyssandra. Marania suspected that she disliked him far more than he disliked her. Still, he rarely betrayed his feelings about much of anything. She reached for one of the books that constantly littered the head table, save for banquet evenings, and observed her late sister's husband out of the corner of her eye as she absently flipped through the pages.

Steflan had been rather handsome when he was younger, but the stress of ruling the kingdom and raising his young son alone over the past year had taken its toll. The bags under his eyes were heavy and gave him the appearance of constant fatigue. His once dark auburn hair was graying at the temples, and his frame had become relatively thin and frail as his physical activity decreased. He looked well past his thirty-five years of age.

Marania watched as the king absently reached over to the next chair and ruffled the little prince's chestnut brown hair. Despite looking distracted by his toy soldiers, everyone knew the boy was listening to his father's every word. At eight years of age, he should have been actively learning to be a leader and warrior himself one day. However, the once active and outspoken child had not uttered a single word since his mother died. Marania hated that. Her bright nephew's silence was a constant reminder of her terrible deed. Fortunately, she wouldn't have to deal with that much longer.

The boy caught his aunt's gaze with his brown eyes and smiled shyly at her by way of greeting. A pang of guilt hit her stomach as she smiled back. He looked so much like her sister, unlike Marania herself, blonde-haired and green-eyed as she was. She tried to turn her attention to her book, wanting to appear calm when news of a visitor arrived. Failing to concentrate on the words in front of her, she found her ears preoccupied with the conversation at the other end of the table. Everything she could make out was about the council meeting the previous morning. Annoyingly, the king and his lords were doing their best to keep the conversation between themselves.

As Marania was straining to listen in, old Hemsgrid hurried into the room, his breath short and his words flustered. The king looked up at his wiry chief advisor and furrowed his brows. "Hemsgrid, whatever is the matter? You look as if you've seen a ghost."

"Well...sire, I regret to inform you that..." Hemsgrid was hardly able to get the words out.

Steflan stood and put his hands on his old friend's shoulders, steadying him. "Pull yourself together, man. What is it you're trying to tell me?"

Hemsgrid took a deep breath. As he was about to continue, Zepatra swept into the room, looking quite intimidating despite her walking stick.

Oldart stumbled in behind her, visibly annoyed. "I'm sorry, Your Majesty. I tried to stop her."

"As did I," Hemsgrid interjected. "She insisted, and well...you know the effect her people can have..."

"I certainly do." The king's square jaw was rigid, and he stared coldly at the Havani woman. "Zepatra," he said, entirely unamused. "What are you doing here?"

Marania stood up in alarm and tried to appear unfazed. "You know this woman, brother?" She furiously made eye contact with Zepatra. This was not part of the plan.

"Oh, we're acquainted," the old woman said with a sly smile. She looked around at the assembly and paused as she caught sight of the prince, who had gotten out of his chair to take cover behind his father. "Well, who do we have here?" The boy glared nervously at the woman before them.

King Steflan did not revert his gaze from Zepatra. "Marania, would you leave us, please? You as well, my lords." He gestured to the others in the room.

The duchess frowned. "Steflan, I really don't–"

"Out!" He cut her off, clenching his fists.

Marania bit her tongue and left the room in a huff, the two lords following her. Oldart and Hemsgrid stayed and pushed the grand double doors shut behind them. The whispering courtiers shuffled down the passage, disappearing around a corner. The duchess remained just outside the great hall, pacing nervously back and forth. *Who does he think he is? Who does SHE think she is?*

When Marania had visited the fortune teller's shop in the village, the old hag had neglected to mention that she knew the king. What else had the Havani kept from her? This development could ruin her plans. Everything had happened so abruptly, and she'd lost control. If this didn't work, what would she tell Lord Kels and Lady Enid when she spoke to them in the morning? She'd assured them she could do this herself. Talis, as she'd eventually learned to call him, and the rest of The Scythe were getting impatient. She felt these were people she didn't want to cross.

Marania was contemplating whether or not to try spying through the keyhole when a loud crash sounded from the room. She jumped as she heard the king roar with anger, and Zepatra burst through the doors.

"Self-fulfilling prophecy!" The crone's voice warned mockingly as she darted past Marania and down the stairs to the foyer.

The duchess fought the urge to follow her and returned to the great hall to find Hemsgrid rubbing his temples. Oldart was sprawled out on the stone floor, looking dazed. The guard stumbled to his feet and ran after Zepatra, barking for any nearby soldiers to join him in his pursuit. A red-faced King Steflan was on his knees helping his son, who had also been knocked off his feet. Despite his defiant expression, the boy was shaking, obviously frightened by the Havani madwoman and his father's rage.

Marania stood frozen and shocked in the doorway, transfixed by the conflicted face of her nephew and the fury in Steflan's eyes as he glared past her. After a moment, she let out a sharp breath and left the room. She made her way to her chambers, cursing herself for obeying the king's order to go in the first place and wondering what Zepatra had done to elicit such a reaction. For now, at least, it appeared that whatever events had transpired had accomplished what she wanted. It was time to get a few hours of restless sleep and prepare to carry out the next stage of her plan.

Hours later, Lady Marania cracked open her door and peered into the dark passageway. Most of the torches had burned out, and the only light came from the open foyer below, which was still under guard from the earlier events of the evening. The maids told her that Zepatra had been followed by Oldart and his men, but there had been no sign of her past the main gate. If they couldn't capture her, they at least wanted to be definite that she didn't return. In the chaos of her exit, Marania had forgotten her promise to ensure Zepatra wasn't followed by the guards. Even without that help, she felt confident the Havani woman had made her escape and left Enderhail far behind.

She took a shaking breath as she pulled up her hood and stepped out of her chambers, silently closing the door behind her. The thought of the next terrible deed she would carry out gave her pause, if only for a moment. Despite the things she had already done, this would undoubtedly be the most challenging part of her plan.

Marania shuddered and pressed forward, taking a right turn down the hall toward the king's chambers. Upon reaching the first door, she pressed her trembling hand against the wood and closed her eyes with a deep sigh. The late queen's chambers had not been touched in a year. The events of that night threatened to overwhelm her, but she took a quivering breath and steeled herself, moving on to the next door.

Very slowly, Marania pushed the king's door open and slipped into the large room. The fire was on its last embers and cast shadows all over the high ceilings. She looked over at the large four-poster bed where the king slept, shaking her head and scoffing silently. She could take him out of the equation at that very moment if she wanted to. Part of her did want to, in fact. It would be so simple. However, she and The Scythe had something else in mind for Steflan, an end that would require more patience and cunning than merely slitting his throat. For that reason, she would ignore this particular murderous impulse, for the time being at least. *Enjoy the time you have left, Your Majesty,* she thought bitterly. *However long that may be.*

Having satisfied her perhaps infantile desire to mock the sleeping monarch, she turned to the small bed on the other side of the room. The little prince lay fast asleep, a ratty blue blanket cradled tightly in his arms. It was unusual for a king to share a chamber with his young child, but after what had happened to the queen, he wanted to keep his son close by. *Understandable and yet utterly inconvenient.*

Marania sighed heavily and softened her gaze as she looked at the boy. Part of her wished it did not have to be this way. But there was no other option. She gently picked up the child, grunting under his weight, and checked that the blanket was not left behind. Despite the nightly sleeping draught he was given to keep his nightmares at bay, she feared he would make a fuss if it left his grasp. It was the only thing he had of his mother's.

Carrying the boy in her arms, the duchess silently left the room and crept back into the corridor. Feeling along the dark wall as she walked, her hand found the latch to the small door leading to the servants' back staircase. To her alarm, the hinges let out an ear-shattering squeal. She froze, teeth gritted. She didn't dare move another inch until she knew it hadn't been heard by the guards in the open foyer below. A strained few seconds passed without a sign of movement from any direction. When she was satisfied with the silence, she carefully closed the door and continued her journey. She padded down the drafty staircase to the kitchens, which were thankfully deserted and had an outside door leading to the back of the courtyard.

When Marania finally stepped into the cold night air, she heaved a sigh of relief and instinctively held the boy closer. The night guards were already giving up their posts and gravitating towards their warm beds in the barracks, just as a recent Scythe recruit from the army had told her. Steflan would certainly be enraged to know his men were neglecting their duties, but it meant that no one was there to question or stop her. She crossed the empty courtyard as quickly as possible and ran down the hill to the tree line, as far into the forest as she dared this late at night. The weight of the child in her arms slowed her a bit, but not enough to deter her convictions. A bright, full moon made the frost shine on the fallen leaves and lit her way through the twisted branches and low underbrush.

Finding a well-hidden hollow in the trees, she set her nephew softly on the forest floor and knelt beside him. Her hand disappeared into her cloak and produced her dagger, shaking so hard she could barely hold it steady. *You've got to do this, Marania. You've done it before, with this very knife. This is your last step. Everything else will be easy from here.* She closed her eyes and raised the quivering blade above her head, intending to plunge it downward before she could even think about stopping herself.

As she was about to do just that, the boy sighed and stirred, causing his aunt to open her eyes. He smiled in his sleep and curled himself into a ball, his hair falling across his face. His mother had often slept like that as a child.

Tears instantly filled Marania's eyes, her trembling arm stuck in the attack position as her heart fought what her brain was telling it to do. She didn't even realize she'd released her grip until the knife hit the ground with a dull thud. Why was this time so much harder? She stared at the child, swallowing her sobs and shivering from cold and anxiety. Several minutes passed before the fog of dread cleared from her brain, and her breathing returned to normal.

Suddenly overcome with nostalgia, she began a lullaby, one her mother used to sing to her and her sister when they were young. As she sang the comforting words, she reached out to stroke the boy's hair. His eyes opened slightly at her touch, startling his aunt. She stopped and held her breath, slowly moving her hand away and hoping he wouldn't wake. The child didn't stir again, his brown eyes fluttering closed. Feeling a strange combination of relief and disappointment, Marania reached for her dropped dagger and forced herself to stand and back away, leaving her nephew alone in the night.

She made her lonely way back to the castle, through the kitchens, up the stairs, and down the hall to her chamber. The bed was warm and inviting; the fire in her room had not yet died down. She collapsed on the blankets and closed her heavy eyelids. The image of the sleeping boy burned in her mind. It was done. Surely, the child would die in no time out there on his own. His blood would not be on her hands. He would simply be another victim of the harsh Enderhail weather. The Scythe had told her this was another necessary sacrifice, and she knew they were right. They didn't need to know how she had done it. All they had to do now was wait for the inevitable. Once the prince's body was found, the king would do the rest of the damage himself. It was only a matter of time.

Back in the forest, the sun had barely begun to rise. In the dim morning light, the little prince finally shivered himself out of his sleep. He peered around blearily and sat up in confusion. He didn't know where he was or how he had gotten there. He didn't know where his father was. He got up slowly, struggling to make out his unfamiliar surroundings. A wolf howled in the distance, chilling the boy to his very bones. He dashed in the opposite direction, his tattered blanket clutched tightly to his chest. After several minutes, he turned to look behind him and careened into a fallen tree. Flipping head over heels and hitting the ground with a terrible thud, the world around him turned to total darkness. He felt a wave of calm wash over him as he slipped into unconsciousness.

Chapter Two

"*ATTENTION: The people known as the Havani have been identified as a threat to the safety of the Kingdom of Enderhail. Any and all Havani are to be arrested on sight and brought to the castle for questioning. Any resistance by the people in question will not be tolerated. Those wishing to join the Royal Inquisition Force should immediately report to the castle barracks. Ten silver pieces will be rewarded for each day of service until the time when the task is completed. Enderen citizens found to be aiding and abetting those of the Havani race will be charged with treason and punished accordingly.*
By order of King Steflan Felhold"
-Notice from the castle

As the morning mists began to settle, light autumn snow fell on the Havani caravan that had concealed itself in this corner of the forest, backed up against a river. The air buzzed with nervous tension and low voices as the group quietly and efficiently broke camp once again. The ability to move quickly had thus far kept them out of harm's way. No one was eager to break that pattern.

Amid the bustle, Chief Rafayel Fortista sat on the driver's seat of his wagon. The man's worried blue eyes surveyed the crowd as he tried to organize the cacophony of unsettling thoughts. His rough and weathered hands clutched a crumpled sheet of parchment that had been brought to him by one of his scouts the night before, stolen off the wall of the guard house in the nearest village. He had read it so many times in the past ten hours that he had memorized the chilling words.

Rafayel had known things were bad for the past week, but this notice changed everything. Now, the threat was real. He had to keep his people safe at all costs. At the moment, he wasn't sure how to accomplish that goal. Enderhail's mountainous borders boasted only one passable route into the next kingdom, which had likely been closed already. The rest of the range was impenetrable. He supposed all they could do at this point was change locations as often as possible and try to fight if and when necessary. Moving was easy for a race of peaceful nomads. Fighting was the far more daunting task.

His thoughts were interrupted by a hand slapping his knee. "Are you alright, Raf? You look like you've gotten lost in your little world, my friend."

Fortista blinked and turned to face Sertus, his head scout and closest comrade. "Oh, how I wish that were all." He shoved the notice into the pocket of his long coat and jumped off the wagon. The two men started rounding the encampment and observing the packing. "Have you been able to find out anything else?"

"A bit," Sertus replied thoughtfully. "You haven't heard of this Zepatra woman, have you?" Rumors had been flying around the kingdom for days now. Still, they'd been able to piece together precious few accurate details of the troubling situation.

The chief raised an eyebrow. "Quite an unusual name, I must say, even for our people. No, I'd never heard of her."

The scout chuckled. "I thought not. The trouble is, it seems no one else has either. None of the tribes our scouts have contacted know who she is or what tribe she originally came from."

"And you say she's been living in the village near the castle?" the chief asked.

"Oh yes, for many, many years. In fact, Zepatra is rather famous for her supposed ability to tell fortunes. Apparently, people came from miles around seeking her aid and willing to pay a pretty penny for it."

Rafayel rolled his eyes. "Do we know for a fact that she's a Seer?" It was unlikely, but not impossible. That was how the raids had started, after all; the king's men began by searching out those with the ability unique to their race, and they'd only resorted to violence upon meeting resistance. At least, that's how things had been up until now.

"Well, she claimed to be," Sertus replied incredulously. "You know as well as I do how rare that is. She likely just knew what to say to swindle some of the more superstitious Enderens. Unfortunately, one of those irrational souls was the king."

Rafayel felt his stomach tighten and groaned in exasperation. "By The Seven Sorcerers, why would she be fool enough to do that? Doesn't she know how that sorry excuse for a leader views us? No wonder things have gone so wrong so quickly."

"There's more..." Sertus sounded pained at the prospect of telling him.

Fortista paused and turned to face his friend, hands clasped behind his back and tension creeping into his voice. "Well, I don't have all day."

Sertus sniffed loudly and blinked several times, apparently searching for the right words. "Well, uh, not only did this woman successfully deceive the king, it appears that she returned to the castle later that night and took his son."

Chief Fortista's jaw dropped, and he stilled, his eyes hardening as his thoughts raced through the implications. The hair on Sertus's arms raised as an almost physical chill swept between the two men. He'd never been on the receiving end of the chief's quiet ferocity and was glad of it. It was both fascinating and utterly terrifying.

Sertus put a hand on the chief's shoulder. "I understand. Believe me, I do. But it's happened. We can't do anything about it. All we *can* do now is try to keep our people safe. I took the liberty of checking on the nearest tribes, and they're fine for now. Perhaps we should consider banding all your tribes together. Safety in numbers and all that."

"Safety in numbers, yes," Raf confirmed. "However, the *speed* in numbers is less than ideal. We should stick to our smaller groups until we can more accurately assess the threat." He took a deep breath and grasped his companion's shoulder. "Thank you, Sertus, you've been most helpful. Go, see to your family's needs."

Sertus bowed his head with a small smile and took his leave, quickly heading for a wagon on the opposite side of the encampment.

Rafayel stared after him for a long moment and groaned, closing his eyes. "Of all the..." he launched into a quiet but vigorous string of expletives in both the seldom-used Havani language and Enderen. He knew it wouldn't help, but it would make him feel better, at least for a while. As he continued with his crass monologue, he felt his stress begin to fade away. That is until another voice reached his ears.

"Papa?"

He stopped abruptly and felt his face go flush. Keeping his head level, he slowly shifted his gaze downward to find his small daughter staring up at him, a wide-eyed and concerned expression clouding her little face. He found himself groaning internally. Of course, she had to approach him in his moment of foul-mouthed weakness. As usual, her timing was impeccable.

The chief forced a smile and knelt down so he was face-to-face with her. Xanya was small for her eight years of age but strong in heart and spirit. Her raven black hair and fair skin mirrored that of the rest of her race. Her eyes, however, were a rare piercing violet rather than the usual blue. The only other person Rafayel had known with those eyes was his late lamented wife. It might as well have been Ravenia's face staring up at him rather than that of the child she bore. His heart couldn't have stung more if someone pierced it with a dull dagger.

The little girl furrowed her brows and folded her arms. "Mama wouldn't want you to talk that way," she chastised gently.

The chief hung his head with a sheepish smile, then looked up and tweaked his daughter's nose. "No, I don't suppose she would. Thank you for reminding me."

"Papa, what's going to happen to us?"

Rafayel's heart sank. He'd wanted to spare her the details, but Xanya had always been a perceptive child. She would learn sooner or later. He wanted her to hear it from him. If only his wife were still here...

"I don't know, child. I'm sorry, but I truly don't. There are some very powerful people who want to hurt us. I don't know if I'll be able to stop them. I promise you this: I will do everything possible to keep you safe. Do you believe me?"

Xanya's bright eyes were clouded with sadness, but she nodded and reached to give him a hug. He took the girl in his arms and held her tightly for a few moments. If only that action alone could protect her from whatever might be coming. She was young and frightened, but he knew she understood and trusted her father.

She pulled away and squeezed his hands with her little fingers. "I have all my things packed in the wagon."

"Good girl. Now run along and see if you can help the others." The chief watched her trot across the camp and begin helping other families load their belongings. Xanya was headstrong, self-sufficient, and resourceful, as all Havani children were raised to be. Their way of life needed a certain hardiness. But she also had a compassionate nature, just like her poor mother. He'd failed to protect his beloved wife. He did not intend to do the same with what he had left of her.

As the chief watched, Xanya suddenly stopped what she was doing and whirled around, her eyes wide with alarm. "Papa!" Her distressed cry shattered the silence of the woods.

A shout came through the trees, and Bram, one of their scouts, came barreling into view. "They're coming! Grab the horses! Run!"

Rafayel turned in time to watch the scout fall to his knees, an arrow protruding from his back. The chief ran to his tribesman and dropped to the ground beside him. Bram was barely breathing; he must have been hit before he came rushing back.

A second arrow, doused in flames, came sailing out of the fog and set the nearest wagon ablaze. Through the blaze and the smoke, the chief stared in horror as a battalion of the king's mounted soldiers rode into the clearing. "RUN!" He bellowed over the rising screams. He frantically scanned the clearing for Xanya, but she had already been caught up in the commotion. *Someone will grab her. She'll be alright.* He scrambled to their wagon for his rarely used sword, just in time to stop a blow from a sneering soldier.

The soldiers were merciless, starting fires, pillaging, and cutting down anyone who crossed their paths. The Havani had scattered, some grabbing weapons, others clutching prized possessions and attempting to flee, and some falling to the ground dead. Many of the nomads had never been forced to defend themselves in such a way, and it was painfully clear that they were severely outnumbered and outmatched. Despite these handicaps, the members of this proud tribe were not willing to resign themselves to death. If the choice was fight or die, they would gladly fight in any way they could.

Deep in the bedlam, Xanya stumbled through the smoke and haze. She heard the horses screaming and was able to let some loose. If they scattered into the forest, the soldiers might leave them alone. Cries from the nearest tent drew her attention, and she wormed her way through the back, avoiding the crackling flames licking at the walls. Little Koen and his baby sister were sobbing in the corner, all alone and terrified.

What would her father do in this moment? Xanya drew in a sharp breath and instantly started coughing, the smoke filling her lungs. "Come on," she coaxed when she could breathe again. "Let's get you out of here!" She took the younger children by the hand and tugged them outside, desperately looking around for a place to stash them.

There! Just a few yards away were two wagons full of other children and many of the women, guarded fiercely by several tribesmen. Xanya rushed to them, handed off her charges, and attempted to run off again.

"Xanya!" One of the men grabbed her arm. "You need to stay here!"

"No, Perrin!" The little girl jerked away. "I need to find my papa!"

"Xanya!" Perrin was pulled into a skirmish with a few of the soldiers before he could continue to protest.

The chief's daughter frantically searched for her father. Where was he? She listened for his voice in the clamor of shouting, screaming, and clanging swords. She headed toward where she'd last seen him, her heart hammering in her chest. The tears she could no longer hold back began to stream down her face. "Papa! Where are you?" She cried as she dashed through the chaotic scene.

In her disorientation, the tiny girl slammed into a spooked horse. She was roughly thrown to the ground beside another wagon, gasping for breath. As the animal galloped off and Xanya tried to get up, a soldier stepped on her woolen cloak, forcing her back to the forest floor. He was a tall, ugly brute with a large nose and pock marks scarring his wind-burned face. This man had probably been in more battles than he remembered, and his armor was scuffed and dented. He sneered smugly at the child and raised his sword dramatically, preparing to plunge it into her tiny chest.

Xanya closed her eyes and took a deep breath, her heart pounding in her ears. *I can't die like this, not now.* She turned her face to the ground under the wagon, not wanting to watch. And yet...something in her gut told her to open her eyes again. They widened as they caught sight of a sword lying on the damp earth. In a split second, she reached for it, not knowing if she would even be able to lift it but knowing she had to try. The weapon was surprisingly light, and without thinking, she thrust it upward, between the pieces of aged armor and into the unsuspecting soldier's soft abdomen.

His sneer slackened into a look of shock and pain, and he fell forward. The girl screamed and rolled to the side before he could crush her. She slowly got to her feet and studied the fallen man. He was dead. She had killed someone. Acrid bile made its way into her throat, and she quickly forced it back down. Everything suddenly went numb. The corpse swam before her eyes, blurring into the muddied ground.

When she was finally able to tear her gaze from the body, Xanya looked around at the battle unfolding before her, her mind disoriented. So many of her people lay dying on the frozen ground. The flames were destroying their belongings. She still had no idea where her father was or if he was even alive.

She heard a familiar cry of pain sound from across the clearing. Xanya turned towards the noise and stared in alarm through the swirling smoke. Everything else seemed to stop as she saw her father fall to the ground, his face screwed up in agony. The soldier standing over him continued to beat him with his sword. She screamed again, and her tears turned from those of fear to anger and grief. There was no way she could safely get to him. In her young heart, she was sure he wouldn't survive the beating he was taking. She started gasping for breath, the world around her again blurring into nothingness. Dazed, the child turned to the blood-stained sword in her hand. She had to get away. To survive.

Without a second thought, she shoved the weapon into her belt and turned away from the stench of death. She dashed from the mayhem into the shelter of the woods, splashing through a shallow part of the river. The only thought in her head was getting as far away from this nightmare as quickly as she could. Her escape went unnoticed by either the soldiers or her tribe.

Meanwhile, the battle was dying down in the gutted encampment, and the remaining soldiers were beginning to retreat. They had lost a fair number of comrades but also cut down many of the Havani. Their king would be pleased with the commander's report. Those with mounts swung themselves back onto their horses, and others took off running into the woods, heading back towards the distant castle. Their sickening cries of victory rang through the trees, taunting the ears of their beaten and innocent victims.

A hyperventilating Chief Fortista slowly opened his eyes and, with great difficulty, attempted to stand. He looked down at his mangled leg and was overcome by nausea. His skin was entirely obscured by all the blood. Another pair of hands struggled to pull him to his feet, and Rafayel turned to see his young niece helping him up. Emmaline smiled sadly at her uncle, still visibly shaken but glad to find him alive. Raf looked around at what was left of his tribe and counted their small number. To his dismay, he had lost more than half of his charges. He knew they would rebuild in time, but the scars of the day's battle would likely never heal.

Suddenly, his mind cleared, and he turned to Emmaline frantically. "Where is she? Where's Xanya?" He grabbed her shoulders and repeated the question.

Emmaline began to cry. She was several years older than Xanya, but the two were as close as sisters. The girl clearly dreaded what she had to tell the injured and terrified man.

"I am so sorry, Uncle. She wasn't with the other children. I-" she stuttered through her tears. "I am so, so sorry..."

The color drained from Fortista's already pale face. He let go of Emmaline, hobbling through the ruins and calling desperately for his child, scanning the lifeless faces on the ground. Those Havani who were left had not seen her, and she was not among the dead. Perhaps the king's men had taken her. Maybe she had burned to death, and her body was no longer recognizable. She could have run away and fallen to some fatal wound. Whatever the reason, his daughter was gone. Rafayel was now alone in the world.

As his remaining subjects numbly began to prepare their dead for burial and gather what was left of their belongings, Fortista dropped to his knees and wept, his whole body shaking uncontrollably. His sobs echoed beyond the boundary of the camp, piercing the already broken hearts of the members of his tribe. There was nothing left for him now.

Hours later, in the dark of the night, little Xanya settled into a large hole in a tall old tree. It was as high as she dared climb. It was cold, but she hoped that the small space would warm her and allow her to get some sleep. She had wandered several miles from the camp, never letting her blade leave her hand. She didn't know where she was going but wanted to get as far away as possible. So far, she still didn't have a plan. She didn't even know if or where she could be safe. At the moment, she was too tired and shaken to formulate anything resembling a coherent thought. She supposed she should wait until morning and look at things in the light of a new day. As she drifted off, she said the traditional burial prayers for her father and the rest of her tribe. If she were to die now, at least she would be able to see them all again.

Chapter Three

"Children are far wiser and more resourceful than we give them credit for. I often wonder what could become of the kingdom if I were to let my own daughters run the council meetings. What creative ideas might spring from their beautiful young minds!"

-Journal entry from the late King Thane Donavar

Xanya crawled out of her shallow cave, rubbed the sleep from her eyes, and looked around the clearing before her. A breeze swept through the air, forcing her to pull her cloak tighter around her shivering body, though the garment did little to fight off the chill. She should be used to the cold, she thought. After all, she'd spent her whole life in these woods. This, however, was different. She no longer had the protection of her tribal family to keep her warm and safe. For the first time in her life, she was alone.

Her little fingers shook in the cold, but eventually, she managed to restart the fire that had blown out during the night. Comforted by the flames and with nothing more to do for the moment, she sat in the crisp morning air and surveyed her surroundings. The rising sun filtered through the trees and shone pinpricks of light on the red and yellow leaves that littered the ground. Though she loved the snow that would soon cover all of Enderhail, this short-lived autumn season was the girl's favorite.

Seven long and lonely days had passed since Xanya ran away from the remnants of her tribe. She traveled as far as she could during that time, though continued sightings of the king's men had led her to spend some of it in hiding. The cave, which she'd found two nights before, had seemed like a comfortable place to rest and decide what to do. After all, she hadn't exactly *planned* on running away. Where could she possibly go now? Another Havani tribe would likely take her in, perhaps even try to get her home. But even if she did come across another tribe, would she be able to get through another ambush? She'd survived the first one; it wasn't likely she'd be that lucky again.

She glanced at the sword sitting on the ground beside her and once again picked it up to study it. She had never seen such a beautiful weapon. Intricate designs were etched into the silver blade, and a polished emerald was set in the hilt. It was strangely light enough for even her to wield and yet sturdy enough to be effective in battle. To her knowledge, none of her fellow tribesmen had owned such a blade. Yet it somehow had to have been under that wagon before the soldiers arrived. There was no other explanation. She supposed it was not important. Nonetheless, it puzzled her.

Her thoughts turned to the events of that dark day and the last words her father had spoken to her. She supposed she could be angry. He had not kept his word to keep them safe. Still, she knew it wasn't his fault. None of it mattered now, anyway.

A nearby bird call pulled her out of her memories, and she shook herself back to reality. Xanya stood, tucked the sword into her belt, and made her way to the nearby creek, where she washed her face in the frigid water and ran her wet hands through her long black hair. She quickly plaited it out of her face and headed towards the first of a few traps she had set over the last couple of days. There had been a few meager meals in the bag she had on her person when she ran away, but those had quickly disappeared. Today, she might have caught a rabbit or squirrel to quell her growing hunger if she was lucky.

The first two traps yielded nothing, but she had higher hopes for the one that was farthest from her cave. As she got closer, she heard a loud rustling through the trees. *Success!* The girl slowed her pace, trying not to make a sound as she rounded the small hill that hid the last of her traps.

She gasped and jumped, taken aback by what she saw. A scrawny boy about her age was stuck upside down in the trap, his left leg bleeding. He was struggling with the branches and looked up in surprise as he heard her approach. Xanya had seen Enderens before; their skin was light, though more pink than hers, but something about this boy's rich brown hair and eyes struck her. She ran forward to help him untangle and stand, examining his wound as she did so.

"Are you alright?" Xanya's little voice cracked. This was the first time she had spoken in days. The boy glared at her and started to back away. "No, don't worry," she offered, her voice stronger this time. "I can help. If you follow me, I'll clean that for you." She headed back towards the creek, then turned when she didn't hear him behind her. She gave him a small smile and beckoned. "C'mon!" The boy hesitated for a moment, then begrudgingly limped after her.

Once they reached the creek, the boy sat heavily on a rock and let Xanya drip cold water onto his wound. After it was cleaned, the girl tore a small strip of fabric from the bottom of her dress and carefully wrapped his leg. "There," she said confidently, "you'll be fine in a few days." She tried to smile at him again, but he simply stared back, his intense gaze neither friendly nor antagonistic. She studied him closer, taking in his ratty clothes, the frayed blue blanket tied around his neck, and the boots that were too big for him. "Where are you from?" she asked. "Are you lost?"

He still didn't answer. The Havani girl was beginning to get frustrated with her new companion. It was difficult to help someone when they refused to speak to you. She sighed and stood. It was high time she moved on anyway if she didn't want to get caught. "Well, if you are lost, then we can be lost together." She gathered her meager things, checked that her fire was out, and then headed toward where she'd found the boy. She figured he wouldn't want to be left alone and would soon follow if she kept going. It wasn't long before she heard him get up to start after her, and she smiled to herself. It wasn't much, but it was progress.

Most of the day was gone, and the two children were still heading in the same direction through the massive forest. Xanya led the way, although she still had no particular destination in mind. She'd settled on following the creek, which soon turned into a rushing river. If they followed the water long enough, they might find a tribe. It was a risk, but the girl supposed being with other people was safer than wandering alone in the forest.

Throughout the day, the boy had slowly gone from trailing behind Xanya to hobbling beside her. The little Havani girl passed the time by telling him tales of her people. He didn't respond to anything she said but quickly averted his gaze when she occasionally looked over at him. At least he was listening.

Xanya had lost track of the passing hours and suddenly noticed that the light was beginning to fade. It was getting steadily more difficult to see any further than the trees in front of them, and she realized for the first time that day just how hungry she was. She stopped walking and looked around. The boy gave a small grunt as he nearly bumped into her.

"We're going to have to stop for the night." Xanya knelt and started to gather the makings of a fire while the boy nervously kicked at the fallen leaves on the ground. "Do you think you could help? I need two sturdy sticks. There should be some under that fir tree there." She kept her tone friendly but tried to make it clear she was giving an order. If her new friend wasn't going to talk to her, the least he could do was pitch in.

As the boy appeared to take heed of her request, the sound of a breaking branch echoed through the trees. Xanya tensed, drawing her sword from her belt and moving closer to the boy, partially for his protection and partially for her own. Surprisingly, he reached for her wrist and grasped it tightly. After a few moments of silence, a large man burst through the trees. Both children screamed, and the girl raised her blade defensively.

"Boy!" The man cried out in a booming voice and knelt down, reaching toward the young ones. "Where have you been? I've been searching for you all day!" The boy stopped screaming, let go of Xanya, and ran to the stranger, who ruffled his brown hair. "Are you alright?" The boy nodded as Xanya looked on in confusion.

"Sir, who are you, and how did you find us?" she demanded bravely.

"Well, well, well, what do we have here?" The man cocked his head and glanced at the boy. "Where did you find her?"

The boy shrugged dismissively.

Xanya had not yet lowered her weapon. "Answer me!" she pressed. Though she recognized his trapper garb, everything else about this man was foreign to her. His twisted hair was black like hers, but his skin was a beautiful dark brown. As she stared at him warily, a wave of recognition passed over his warm eyes. He started to smile. "... You're a Fortista, aren't you? Rafayel and Ravenia's daughter?"

The girl gasped and slowly lowered her blade at the sound of her parents' names. "How...how do you know who I am?" She had never seen this man in her life.

"My name is Balthazar Gregriss. You wouldn't remember me, child, but your parents and I...we knew each other well. In fact, I was there when you were born. You were so tiny." He smiled playfully and winked at her. "Looks like you haven't changed too much." Balthazar extended his hand, inviting her to come to him.

Xanya smiled despite herself and put her sword back in her belt, taking a few steps forward to place her small pale hand into his dark fingers. For some unknown reason, her fear melted away. Something told her she could trust him.

"Little Xanya Fortista. After all these years, here you are," Balthazar said in a deep, gentle voice, and he looked directly into her eyes. "Your mother had those eyes, you know. I was so very sorry to hear of her passing." His thoughts suddenly appeared far away, and his own eyes began to wander. After a few seconds, he blinked vigorously and shook his head. He fixed his gaze on the girl again with a frown. "Where's your tribe? How did you end up out here all alone?"

Xanya hung her head as the familiar sting of tears welled up in her eyes. "They're... they're gone." She started to sob. The grief she had been pushing aside for survival finally overwhelmed her and came pouring out.

Confused, Balthazar pulled the small girl into his arms and held her tightly, gently rocking her back and forth as the boy looked on. Her words stung his heart. He desperately wanted to know what she meant, but for now, she needed comfort and a warm place to sleep. He was happy to provide both.

CHAPTER FOUR

"Darkness is not always something to run from. Just don't let yourself get so comfortable that you decide to live there."
-Lessons for an Enderen Life, author unknown

It was the middle of the day, but King Steflan's castle was dark, save for the torches that sputtered in the passageways and the large fires that burned in every occupied room. Every window had its thick curtains drawn. It almost seemed the fortress itself was as much in mourning as the people within its walls. The dreary atmosphere was reminiscent of that immediately following the queen's death. If the king was in darkness, he expected everyone and everything else in his world to be in darkness as well.

Despite the suffocating gloom in the household, Lady Marania was feeling rather chipper, more so than she had in a long while. As she passed through the shadowed corridors, she practically had to stop herself from skipping. The Scythe were pleased with her actions, but they were anxious to keep the momentum going. Just as she had predicted, Steflan assumed Zepatra had taken his son. From their brief conversation on the subject, he couldn't work out all the details in his head. He was, however, convinced it could be the only explanation. That was all Marania needed to give him a slight nudge, which she would be all too pleased to do. His reaction to the events of that night couldn't have been more perfect.

Giving a somber nod to some passing ladies in waiting, Marania stopped outside the heavy wooden doors to the great hall, adjusted her black mourning dress, and prepared herself for the performance she'd have to give once she entered. The king was probably sitting on his throne, thinking he would be alone for a while. Meals were currently being served in the library, as he'd ordered. There were no meetings or events planned for the foreseeable future. Why would anyone look for him in there? Apparently, she knew him better than either of them realized.

On the other side of those doors, Steflan did sit on his throne, emotionless and rigid, eyes staring straight ahead. This was the only place he could get away from everyone. There were too many people in this castle, he decided. Too many well-meaning souls were incessantly bringing him things and offering what they believed to be words of comfort. It all felt so empty. He wanted to be in an empty place to embrace the feeling.

The king's head swam with intertwining thoughts: *How did this happen? We had the gates under guard all night. How could she have gotten in? Did she have something to do with Alyssandra's death as well? We never did find out what really happened that night. I should have gone to check on her after supper. Cook went out of his way to make her favorite. When was the last time I ate?*

As if he could no longer hold the weight of his own cluttered mind, Steflan's head finally slumped forward into his hands. What next? Rubbing his eyes in frustration, he supposed he could just sit here in the welcome silence until someone came looking for him. That sounded like the best plan. For the first time in days, he thought the relief of sleep might overtake him and give him a much-needed respite.

As his eyes finally began to droop, an abrupt knock echoed down the length of the chamber. Startled, Steflan growled low and deep in his throat as he slowly looked up, not ready to be disturbed. Then again, he thought, he would probably never be ready. Now was as good a time as any. "Enter." His begrudging voice might have turned anyone else away.

Not the duchess.

Marania pushed on the massive doors, which opened with a resistant squeal, and took a moment to process the dark room. The thick curtains were drawn, no torches were lit, and there was no fire, adding an unwelcoming chill to the space. She could barely make out Steflan sitting at the opposite wall. Carefully stepping forward, she finally found her voice. "Steflan dear, what are you doing sitting here in the dark? Several of us have been looking for you."

Isn't that just lovely? "I wanted to be alone," Steflan grumbled, unimpressed with Marania's familiar tone and lack of decorum.

"Oh, come now, this is no time for gloom." The woman folded her arms and shook her head.

The king grunted. Marania's sickly, sweet voice was annoying him more than usual. Before he could protest any further, the duchess marched boldly into the room. She headed for one of the floor-to-ceiling windows, grabbed a heavy green curtain, and jerked it open. The autumn sunlight outside streamed brilliantly into the space.

Having not seen such light in a few days, Steflan recoiled and covered his eyes with his hands. "What are you doing, woman? You're going to blind me!"

Perhaps that wouldn't be such a bad thing, Marania thought. She soldiered through the rest of the room, pulling open the remaining curtains and waving the falling dust from her face. She finally turned to look at the king, and her voice softened. "It's been a week. You know you can't hide from this forever. The world hasn't stopped. You're still the king, and your people need you." The sentiment was sincere, up to a point. She didn't want the kingdom in complete chaos when she finally assumed the throne. In a strange way, she did feel sorry for him. Though not nearly enough to question her actions.

The king silently rubbed his eyes for a moment, then raised his head and met her gaze with a glare. "I know you're not in the habit of expressing emotion, Marania." Ironically, she had often accused him of the same vice. "But you might have the decency to show *some* concern. After all, it's not just my son who's missing. He's your nephew as well. All that's left of Alyssandra. Don't you care at all?"

An unexpected pang of guilt stabbed Marania right in the stomach. Her inner lightheartedness crumbled at the king's bluntness. She turned back to the nearest window, trying to calm her nerves with the view of the snow-covered mountain peaks. She'd often carried that little boy to these windows to gaze upon the same landscape. As hard as she tried, she'd been unable to rid her mind of every memory, just like with her sister.

Marania was also somewhat concerned that the child's body had not been found. She'd left him in that exact spot for that very purpose. It was lucky Steflan jumped to the conclusion that he did, but still, a corpse would have given her more assurance. Where had the boy gone? What would she do if he suddenly wandered into the castle? *No, it's too late for second thoughts. Put on the act.*

When she finally turned back to Steflan, she slowly approached him. "Of course, I'm concerned. I'm sorry. You know how dearly I love that child. It would kill me if anything happened to him." She was only half lying. Despite everything, she did regret that her sister's son had to become a pawn in this deadly game she was playing. "However, I don't think stagnation is the best way to handle the situation. Oldart and his men are doing everything possible to get him back and dispense justice to the responsible parties. Even if, heaven forbid, we don't find him, at least you know the Havani won't soon forget your wrath."

She had initially suggested hunting down only the Seers and having them disposed of if they couldn't supply information. They, unfortunately, had proved difficult to pick out of the crowd, and none had been willing to betray their fellow tribesmen. After that, things quickly escalated into full-scale attacks. Marania wasn't sure how to stop it. When she'd mentioned the assaults to The Scythe, they'd all been wholly dismissive and told her not to be bothered by a few more dead nomads. So there she'd left it. If Talis and his minions didn't mind, neither did she.

"It's not likely that Zepatra could have left the kingdom with the prince. If he's still alive, we'll find him somewhere. I'm sure of it." She ascended the small set of stairs to his throne to place a comforting hand on Steflan shoulder. Predictably, he tensed at her touch. Most families would have come together in such times of hardship. Not this one.

Even from their first introduction, Steflan and Marania had merely tolerated one another's presence. Perhaps, at first, she had been jealous that her father had gone out of his way to bring the younger Alyss such a handsome and capable husband, leaving her to become a spinster. Looking for Steflan's flaws had been a way to dispel those feelings of envy. After a while, she could see nothing else. And he had immediately noticed the air of pretension that exuded from Marania, the magnitude of which was unbecoming even for a royal. Her posturing had only become more evident and unappealing as they got older. He supposed they would have to find a way to cope with one another as the only remaining royals. That was easier said than done.

Steflan cleared his throat and, in an awkward attempt to diffuse the palpable tension, gingerly patted Marania's fingers in thanks. She immediately withdrew her hand and tried not to let revulsion creep into her small smile. This was not how she had intended the conversation to go. Thankfully, Hemsgrid then entered the room with a bow and gave her an excuse to back away.

"Majesty, some of the troops have returned from raids and are eager to give their reports. We also have some new recruits awaiting your inspection. Would you like to attend to these matters now, or shall I tell Oldart to have the men stand down for the afternoon?"

Steflan sighed. No, he did not wish to attend to these matters now. The recruits could wait forever for all he cared. He wanted nothing more than to sit alone in the dark with his tortured thoughts. Or possibly tear the kingdom apart looking for his child. Unfortunately, it seemed his time for grief had ended. Duty called. As much as he hated to admit it, Marania was right. The world had not stopped, and this corner of it depended on his leadership.

After a long pause, he stood and addressed his advisor. "Fetch my council, Hemsgrid. Have them meet Oldart and myself at the barracks. I have not yet received word of how our operations are proceeding, and I'm eager for the information." He descended the stairs and approached the wiry older man. "We should also do what we can to ensure that the details of the prince's absence remain unknown. If that wretch does indeed have him and hasn't left the kingdom, we don't want to arouse any suspicion or alarm. When we do find them, we'll catch her by surprise."

Steflan then strode towards the open doors and shot an emotionless glance at Marania as he passed, unsure about their interaction. He made a mental note to keep a closer eye on her. Why he felt that necessary, he couldn't say. For the time being, he had other matters on his mind. He turned his attention to Hemsgrid, who hadn't wasted a moment sharing the news he was privy to.

If the king had indeed kept an eye on Marania, he might have noticed her trailing behind him through the corridors, whispering to a few passers-by along the way. By the time Steflan reached the courtyard, several of his courtiers had slipped into a side hallway and made their way down to the old dungeon, where the growing Scythe of Dormastis was eagerly assembling to hear their own report from the treacherous sister of the late queen.

Chapter Five

"Have the strength to find stability in whatever circumstance you may find yourself. This is a lesson our child must learn if she is to thrive in this changing world."

-Letter from Ravenia Fortista to her husband, Rafayel

Xanya sat at Balthazar's sturdy table in his cozy trapping cabin, enjoying her first decent meal in several days. The venison stew he had prepared was exactly what she needed to clear her head. She had even begun to enjoy herself a bit. Though still grieving for her family, she could already feel the stress and loneliness from the last few days melting away. She licked her wooden spoon clean and set it in her empty bowl. "Could I have some more, please?"

Balthazar smiled and took Xanya's bowl. As he carried it back to the boiling pot hanging over the fire, he wondered again why Xanya had been alone in the woods. Her statement that her tribe was "gone" had haunted him all evening. Despite his strong feelings that something was terribly wrong, he wanted the girl to feel safe and comfortable with him before pressing the subject further.

As Balthazar busied himself with the food, Xanya took her first good look around the large main room of the cabin. The tall walls were made of stout logs that had been hand-cut and girdled, then stacked snugly to keep out the elements. Small torches lined the walls, illuminating the stacks of pelts and various tools of the trapper trade that hung from hooks all around. On one side of the sloped ceiling was a small loft accessible by a ladder, underneath which was an open doorway leading to another room. Having spent her whole life traveling in and living out of a wagon, this was the first time Xanya had been in a house. She decided she liked it.

Since they'd arrived at Balthazar's home, Xanya had tried to avoid the pair of brown eyes staring intently at her from across the table. It wasn't that the boy made her uncomfortable. She just couldn't figure him out. All the Havani children she had grown up with were outgoing, talkative, and energetic. So far, this boy was the opposite of all those things. It made her wonder where he had come from and what sort of family he had. Did he have friends he played with? Did they miss him? Xanya had been devastated when she had to run from her family. Based on his behavior, it was hard to tell if the boy had anyone he missed. Until now, he'd been acting more nervous than sad or frightened.

This is silly, Xanya finally thought. *He can't be that different from me.* For the first time since entering the house, she looked directly at the boy and tried to offer him a small smile. His blank face stayed still as stone. The girl grunted, furrowing her brows in frustration and concern. "Um, does he speak?" She addressed her guardian hesitantly.

"'Dunno," Balthazar answered. He returned her full dish to the table. "I found him about a week ago, wandering around the woods confused and alone. All he had with him was that old rag." He gestured to the blanket around the boy's neck. "He hasn't said a word to me, but he doesn't seem to want to go anywhere else either. That's fine by me. It's nice to have some company out here. I just wish I knew who he was so I could help him. I'm not even sure he knows that himself."

He shrugged and sat in a fur-lined chair by the fire, reaching for his whittling knife and a gnarled piece of wood.

Those eyes continued to stare at her, and Xanya thought about their day together. When she'd first met the boy, his eyes had been full of fear and mistrust. As they traveled throughout the day, his expression had softened. Still, he'd never given any indication of what he was thinking. It was apparent that he wasn't ready to say anything, if he could even speak at all, so she satisfied herself with just staring back. She narrowed her violet eyes and pursed her lips dramatically, attempting to coax a smile out of him. Nothing. She leaned on her fist and addressed him directly.

"So, do you have a name?" No answer, as expected, but he shrugged his shoulders.

She was finally getting somewhere. At least he was acknowledging her. "Is there...a name you would like to be called?"

The boy's face became thoughtful, his downcast eyes seemingly searching for something. Then, he abruptly shook his head and stared at the floor.

"Hmm..." Xanya glanced at Balthazar, who had looked up from his whittling and was curiously watching the interaction between his two young charges.

The Havani girl looked back at the silent child who had followed her through the woods all day. Behind the apprehension, his eyes held a determination and softness, a look that reminded her of her father. Rafayel had instilled in his daughter a strong sense of bravery and compassion. She saw those same traits in the boy across the table. Whatever had happened to him, she wanted him to see her as a friend, to trust her. After all, he'd trusted her enough to follow and listen to her stories all day.

She remembered a theme in stories she'd shared as she thought about their time together. When had the boy been listening most intently? When had she noticed his ears perk up and his eyes sparkle before he quickly looked away from her? Slowly, a memory rose from the depths of her young mind. She glanced back at Balthazar, a genuine smile turning up in the corners of her mouth.

Xanya met the boy's gaze once again. If her working theory was correct, perhaps this would finally work. She spoke softly, recalling details as she went. "When my mother was still alive, my father used to tell us stories of a strong and noble warrior, one who fought bravely and saved many innocent lives from a powerful and unjust ruler. He eventually became a great king and was known the world over for the kindness he showed to his people. He knew the most important thing in a battle was to remember why he was fighting and to show compassion for those who needed it, no matter who they stood for. Would you like to know his name?"

The boy's eyes had lit up during her story, and he nodded eagerly.

"He was called Dominic. It's a good, strong name. I think it could be a good name for you, too...if you would like us to call you that."

The boy appeared lost in thought for a moment. Then he smiled for the first time and got up from his place at the table. He walked around to Xanya's chair and stuck his hand out to her.

"Dominic," he said, his voice small but confident.

Xanya took his outstretched hand and shook it firmly. "Xanya."

As the children grinned at each other, Balthazar leaned forward in his seat and stroked his short beard thoughtfully. He'd been wondering how to entertain them during their stay with him. All this talk of battles and warriors had given him an idea. "Well, it seems I have two little fighters on my hands. Would you like to learn more about that?"

Xanya and Dominic looked at each other and nodded eagerly.

"We can spend some time on that in the morning before I check my traps. For now, finish your meals. I'll make up some sleeping arrangements for you both."

Enderhail's landscape had transformed overnight. The year's first real snow blanketed the kingdom in glistening white drifts, and the faint morning sun provided little warmth from behind the clouds. The kingdom's notoriously long winter had arrived at last.

The sunken glade behind Balthazar's cabin was the perfect setting for two youngsters to learn the art of weaponry and self-defense. If they were to one day survive on their own, it might be necessary for them to be able to handle a blade. Despite being a lone trapper, Balthazar had a rather impressive collection of weapons, and he had selected a few to begin training the children. As the three of them walked outside, he laid them on the ground within a circle of home-made and well-used targets. Practicing his own skills had saved his life more than once.

Though still quiet and slightly wary, Dominic had conversed with others a bit over breakfast that morning and was excited to get started. As he took in the different kinds of weapons being laid out, he play-fully nudged Xanya's shoulder and grinned at her. She noticed how he wrinkled his nose when he smiled like that and couldn't help but smile back. She still knew nothing about him or where he came from but liked that he was opening up a bit. Besides, she was a little excited about the idea of training. Saving herself from that soldier at her camp had been lucky, but she needed to know she could do it again if she had to.

Balthazar finished laying out the weapons. "Alright, you two, the first thing I want you to do is pick a weapon. You could learn them all if you wanted, but becoming highly skilled in one or two is important. I can have you practice some hand-to-hand combat as well, I suppose. You never know when you might lose your weapon. You're both small now, but you could still do considerable damage to an attacker if you know what you're doing. Before we begin, Xanya, there's something I need to know." He pulled her sword from the bag he was carrying and fixed his eyes on her firmly. "Where did you get this?" he asked in a calm but serious manner. "It isn't common for your people to carry weapons, let alone give one to someone as young as yourself."

The girl blinked several times and bit her lip. "Um..." she answered hesitantly, "I...I just found it. I was about to be killed, and just saw it on the ground next to me. I've never seen it before. But it saved my life, and I want to learn how to use it."

Balthazar looked at her thoughtfully, and then his eyes softened. After dinner the previous night, Xanya had volunteered a few details about why she ran away from her tribe. It was no wonder the poor girl was so eager to learn to fight. "Alright, I can teach you. It's a fine blade and should serve you well." He set it aside. "Is there something else you'd like to learn as well?"

Dominic picked up a small spiked mace and swung it around, carefully ducking his head out of the way when necessary. Xanya giggled at his antics and started looking around at the assortment of weaponry, uncertain about some of the pieces she was looking at. Her bright eyes passed over a small bow and quiver of arrows, and she eagerly grabbed for them. Her father had shown her how to shoot a few times. She liked watching the arrows sail smoothly through the air and bury themselves cleanly in their target. It had been a while, but she remembered how to nock an arrow. It wobbled a bit at first, but she soon got it lined up and let the arrow fly. It arched downward and fell feebly into the clean white snow. "Mmm," she growled to herself, frustrated.

"Whoa there, Xanya, let me help you with that." Balthazar strode over and picked the arrow up off the ground. "Good try, but it's all in the posture." He knelt down and handed her the arrow. "Hold the bow in your left hand and nock the arrow with your right." He lined her up with a target, covered the girl's hands with his, and helped her get into position. "Stand as tall as you can, shoulders back. Hold your left arm straight out in front of you. That's it. Then pull the bowstring back with your first two fingers until they just touch your cheek."

Xanya pulled the string back and held it steady.

"Good girl," Balthazar affirmed. "Now you're going to aim, take a deep breath and...loose!"

Xanya's arrow kicked off the string, flew through the air, and hit straight in the bullseye. She let out a whoop, her eyes twinkling with pride and determination. Balthazar backed off and watched her confidently nock another arrow. He smiled to himself as he took the unruly mace from Dominic and handed him a small sword.

Xanya turned triumphantly as she again pierced the target, her little face glowing happily. As he was returning her smile, Balthazar noticed her face fall. Her violet eyes flashed golden as if the flame from a candle flickered behind them for a very brief moment. She ran to Dominic, who had just dropped his sword, and snatched the weapon out of thin air before it sank directly through the top of his foot.

"Be more careful," she warned him sternly, handing the weapon back to the startled boy. "I don't want you to get hurt."

Xanya nodded with satisfaction and marched back to the target, leaving Dominic staring after her in confusion.

Balthazar watched, dumbfounded, as the child returned to her shooting like nothing had happened. *By the Sorcerers, what the...?* The trapper didn't think he'd ever seen anything so strange in his entire life. Strange, but intriguing all the same. Much like the little girl who stood before him.

Chapter Six

"My dear friend,

I wish you could have been here today. Xanya took her first steps! She has so much energy and a bit of a wild, independent streak. I just know things are only going to get harder from here. We have been immensely blessed with this child, and Ravenia and I are so grateful to be her parents. Her kind heart and fiery spirit will make her an excellent leader one day.

As much as I wish I had only good news to share, life in this kingdom has gotten more difficult for our people. We now have limited areas where we can live and travel. Any Havani who dares enter a village is closely observed by castle guards. For security, we're told. The villagers are still kind to us, thank The Sorcerers, but I fear for our future here.

Enderhail is the true home of our people. We cannot abandon our land. But I do sometimes wonder if our brethren in neighboring kingdoms are faced with this kind of persecution. The new king is so unlike his father-in-law, who, as you know, respected our culture and self-sovereignty. Steflan is young and so mistrustful of us. Heaven only knows for what reason. Please let me know if you hear of anything on your travels that may help.

Please come back and visit us soon. We all miss you, your father, and your brother terribly. Our family isn't the same without you. I would love for my child to get to know and love you as we all do.

May The Sorcerers guide you always,

Raf"

-Letter from Rafayel to Balthazar

"The king has wanted to assert dominance over the Havani as long as he's been on the throne, but I never thought he would go this far." Balthazar paced back and forth in front of the fire in his cabin. He'd given Xanya a few days to settle in before asking more questions about the attack. Her story troubled him greatly. His cabin was more than half a day's trek from the nearest village; he had been too busy checking his traps and preparing furs for the coming season to make it to town to hear the latest news. He would have to make a trip in the next few days and see what he could find out. "You're certain your father didn't say anything else to you about the king or the soldiers?"

"No, nothing." Xanya racked her brain, trying to remember any other details. "He was very sad that morning. He didn't tell me why. He probably just didn't want me to worry."

"Do you know how many survivors there were?" Balthazar knew he was probably asking the girl to remember too much, but he needed to find out all he could.

Xanya hung her head. "I ran away while the soldiers were still there. The smoke was too thick to see through, and it was stinging my eyes. When I saw Papa fall, I just wanted to get away." She shrank back in her chair. "There probably weren't very many of them left, anyhow." Her heart still stung with regret for running, though it was far too late for those regrets now. She was alive. At least she could be grateful for that.

She started as a hand grasped her shoulder. Lost in the memories of that terrible day, she'd forgotten Dominic was sitting next to her. Though his shyness had abated a bit over the past few days, he still hadn't said much to either Balthazar or Xanya. Now, here he was, comfortingly squeezing her shoulder and giving her an encouraging smile. Her family was gone. She couldn't change that. But she no longer had to face it alone.

A thought entered her mind, a particular detail she'd forgotten from a previous conversation. "Balthazar, you said you knew my family. And me, when I was very little. But you... don't look like a Havani." She hoped she didn't sound rude. None of the few people she'd met outside of her race looked like Balthazar.

He smiled at her and sat in his fur-lined chair, leaning forward and clasping his rough hands together. "Well, frankly, there aren't very many of the Relkai, my own people, in this kingdom, though my family has lived here for generations. My mother left me and my brother with our father when we were very young. He tried his best to take care of us on his own, but after a few years, he realized it just wasn't enough. Fortunately, he knew some Havani people and was humble enough to ask for their help. Instead of just giving us what we needed, they took us in. No questions asked, no hesitations. I'll never forget the day we packed up what we could carry and left our little house in the village. It was a relief, really. It felt like a chance for a fresh start. The tribe welcomed us with open arms. Someday, you'll learn that most of your people are much more accepting than you realize." He paused, and his eyes sparkled with memories. "Sadly, many Enderens only notice that the Havani are different and are unwilling to understand. That fear keeps them from knowing some of the kindest and most honorable people who've ever lived."

Xanya felt a sudden swell of pride for her people, especially her tribal family. Perhaps she simply hadn't been alive when an outsider had last trusted them enough to ask for help. She liked imagining that her father would have behaved the same way as the chief from Balthazar's story.

The man continued, "Your parents and I were friends from that first day. We played, hunted, worked, did everything together. They meant more to me than anyone else, even to this day. Truth be told, I wouldn't have minded a second glance from Ravenia as we got older, but she only had eyes for Raf. I was far too happy for them to be jealous. Things began to change, though, after your parents married and Raf became chief. Such is the nature of growing up and taking on one's intended responsibilities. I had to decide what I wanted to become and where I wanted to be. The tribe was my life, and I loved it. But I decided it was time for me to see the world beyond these mountains. Trapping was a profession that would allow me to do so. I had all these grand visions of traveling to all the kingdoms and gathering grand stories to bring back home. For a few years, I did just that. I met so many people and learned so much from them. Saw things and places you could never imagine. I even saw the ocean once. It was incredible."

Xanya beamed excitedly. "You've really seen the ocean, Balthazar? What was it like?"

Balthazar leaned back and closed his eyes for a moment. "It was breathtaking. So peaceful and serene. There's nothing like the sound of waves crashing on the shore." He sat up again. "Those years were exciting and new. I could never tell what was going to happen from one day to the next. Part of me wanted it to stay that way forever. But as it turns out, you can't sever your roots that easily. Enderhail was always my home, and I knew I had to return. I came straight back to that little Havani tribe in the forest and was able to be there when you were born." He reached for Xanya's hand, stroking the back of her fingers with his thumb. "Even after I built this cabin and lived on my own, your parents would come to visit occasionally. They brought you a few times, not that you were old enough to remember. I knew they would always be there for me, but things changed after your mother's passing. Raf's visits became less frequent, and he didn't bring you when he did come. Eventually, he stopped coming around altogether. He never mentioned me to you, did he?"

Xanya shook her head sadly. Her father had been a wonderful man and a strong leader, but his grief overshadowed everything he said and did. "I don't have many memories of the three of us together, but I do remember my papa used to laugh and play with us. After my mama died, that stopped. He spent lots of time with me, but he mostly focused on the tribe and never talked about her." She looked at Balthazar thoughtfully before continuing. "I don't think he was trying to shut you out. I think he was just trying to forget the memories."

Balthazar's eyes had grown misty as he stared at the wise little girl sitting across from him. "Perhaps if Raf had not gotten bogged down in his grief, he would have seen the pieces of Ravenia that live on in you."

"What happened to your brother?" Xanya turned in surprise as Dominic asked the question and broke the falling silence. She still wasn't quite used to hearing him speak.

Wiping away his welling tears, Balthazar glanced kindly at Dominic and stood to begin preparing their evening meal. "I'm honestly not sure, son. Our father had died, and I asked him to go with me when I left on my travels. He made it clear he wanted to stay. When I returned, he was gone. No one could tell me where he went, only that he had one day changed his mind. Took off to have his own adventures, I expect. I often wonder about him. If he's still alive, I hope he's safe and happy."

He grunted as he started throwing vegetables into the bubbling pot of melted snow and cleared his throat loudly. "Enough wallowing in the past. It's time we look forward to the future. Now, tomorrow, I'm going to take a little trip into the village to trade some pelts. I'll be gone most of the day, but you two should be perfectly safe here. Hopefully, I'll be able to get some more information about this Havani business. Yours can't be the only tribe that was ambushed unless someone was hiding something. We'll get to the bottom of this and get you both home, don't you worry."

TEN YEARS LATER

CHAPTER SEVEN

"*I was so scared, more scared than I'd ever been. I've always played army games with my friends, but this was nothing like that. These were real weapons, real soldiers who wanted to kill us. My mama grabbed me and tried to run, but she fell, and I got separated from her in the crowd. I called to her, but all the screams drowned me out. The smoke made it hard to see. I was backed up against a huge rock, and there was nowhere to run. When I turned around, a soldier was standing over me. A torch was burning in his hand. He reached down to grab me, but then an arrow hit him in the chest from above, and he fell to the ground. Two figures in black hoods jumped down from the rock, one holding a sword, one a bow. They were fighting the soldiers!*

The one with the bow picked me up and shoved me into a thick bush. A woman's voice came from under the hood and told me to stay there. One by one, the king's men were either killed by these strangers or ran in fear. When the fighting was finally over, the hooded figures talked to the chief and left. I heard whispers among the survivors that this woman was the Huntress, the one we'd been hearing stories of. The one who might finally be able to save us."

-Account from a Havani child survivor

The years passed slowly; the sun rose and set; the seasons flowed from one to another as they always had. And yet, the days seemed interminable. Rafayel Fortista felt that life was something happening to him rather than living it himself. Despite the torment they had endured for the last ten years, he saw joy, love, and laughter in the people of his tribe. He felt none of it.

That first attack on their tribe was a distant blur. Raf remembered only the rush of fear he'd felt when the soldiers had appeared and the grief he'd been saddled with since he noticed Xanya's absence. He stared into the dim morning light and flinched as a twinge of pain crept up his left leg. Even if he somehow managed to push away all the memories, this mangled and scarred limb would never let him ease his burden.

After an initial bout of violence, the attacks had essentially become raids of the tribes. They happened every few weeks, the king's men pillaging camps and forcefully arresting those who resisted. As far as the chief knew, none of those people ever returned home. As the king became more desperate over the years, the raids turned increasingly violent until they were nothing less than massacres.

Rafayel ran his hands through his long dark curls, reached for his crutch, and hobbled out of his tent, wrapping his crimson coat tightly against the chill of the winter air. Even with his injury, he was determined to stand tall and strong. His people not only relied on his leadership for survival; they loved and respected him as well. Making his way around the circle of wagons and tents, as he did every morning, he was greeted by smiles and well wishes from members of his tribe, all of whom he considered friends and family. He recalled the days when he had five tribes under his command, the lower chiefs answering to his leadership, and the joyous gatherings when those tribes came together a few times a year. Those memories sustained him, along with a faint glimmer of hope that they might one day rejoice again as a people. The remaining Havani under his rule were now so few that it had become necessary for them to band together. Sertus' long-ago suggestion of "safety in numbers" finally, and unfortunately, made sense.

As Rafayel continued his morning constitutional, he came upon a young father playing with his little girl. He felt the stab of grief pierce his heart. This family had come to them from the smallest of the Fortista-controlled tribes, severely culled by a recent encounter with the king's soldiers. The man's wife and older son had been killed, leaving him alone to raise his daughter. The child was smiling and laughing, the love for her father shining in her eyes. Rafayel couldn't tear his gaze from the scene. The young man caught him staring and offered the chief a nod and a sad smile. He bowed his head in return and continued on. These two men understood each other in a way they wished they didn't.

Rafayel's thoughts turned to his own daughter, as they often did in these moments. He'd nearly forgotten her face. But he couldn't forget those eyes, the eyes she shared with her mother. They burned in his memory like a flame that couldn't be extinguished. Xanya would be eighteen now, old enough to marry and lead their people. Rafayel didn't think he could have gotten through his early years as chief without Ravenia's wisdom and support. Xanya's husband would have been equally blessed to have her lead by his side.

He finished his rounds and made his way to one of the fires in the center of the encampment, where small clusters were finishing chores, talking, or even softly playing music. Typically, he would have encouraged everyone to make as little noise as possible to avoid attracting attention. But today, in much better times, would have been their

Winter Solstice celebration. They deserved to have at least one element of that joyous day, even if it was just for the morning.

He spotted Emmaline sitting around the largest fire in the center, speaking earnestly with several other women. In the terrible absence of Xanya and her mother, she had taken over what would have been their responsibilities. Leading a tribe was a family effort, and though Emmaline was only his niece, she was his last remaining blood relative. He trusted her with his people and had even considered making her his new heir. That conversation, however, involved several people with whom he was not eager to broach the subject.

Noticing his approach, Emmaline halted her conversation and turned to her chief. "Good morning, Uncle. How are you feeling today?" She asked him this each day without fail, even though she knew the answer.

"I'm alive," his weary reply came as it always did. He winced as the pain crawled up his leg again, and a look of concern fell over Emmaline's face. She took his arm and helped him to sit by the glowing flames.

"It's happening more often, isn't it?" Her question was more of a statement than anything else. "Have you been to see the healer?"

"More times than I can count," he replied. "She knows nothing can be done. We may as well chop it off and pray I don't bleed out."

The young woman cringed at the thought. "Please don't talk like that. It doesn't help."

"I know, I know," Rafayel grumbled and rolled his eyes, which caught Emmaline's hard stare. "I'm sorry, I just... she's really been on my mind lately."

Emmaline sat next to him and pulled her knees up to her chin. "Mine too. She was my best friend, you know. No one had a heart like hers. If I may say so, Aunt Ravenia would have been proud of how you raised her."

Rafayel blinked away the tears that were starting to fill his eyes and cleared his throat loudly. Emmaline's words meant a great deal to him, but this life left little room for sentimentality. He had to be resilient for his people. Most of the time, that meant pushing away the past and facing the future one day at a time. He gave his niece a small smile and turned the conversation to the business at hand. "Are we ready to break camp at first light tomorrow? We've been here too long. It's time to move on to the next stop; leave this one for another tribe."

"Yes, sir, everything is in order. Everyone knows their duties, and they're always ready to go." Emmaline stood and placed a comforting hand on his shoulder. "We've done this hundreds of times now," she said reassuringly. "We always know what to do. Nothing will go wrong."

The chief nodded and gently tweaked her nose. "Thank you, dear."

She was right. There was no reason to believe anything would go wrong, at least for now. Raf had developed this network of hiding places himself. These large open spaces were well hidden in the forest and away from the prying eyes of outsiders. Many remaining tribes had been using this same travel system for the past few years. The attacks, brutal as they were, had become less frequent thanks to Chief Rafayel Fortista. If a camp was found by the king's men, it was scrubbed from the map, and a red scarf was left behind, tied to a tree. The scarf let any incoming tribes know that that particular location was no longer safe. It was, Raf believed, his most significant achievement as a leader. Regrettably, it couldn't bring back everything they'd already lost.

He turned to the rest of the crowd and began softly singing along with their tune. The man rarely felt at peace anymore. But now, just for a moment, he tried to be in the present and enjoy himself. The song was gentle and slow, a reminder of their past and a tenuous hope for the future. Just as he was getting lost in the music, a branch rustled behind him, and he turned to see one of his night scouts come slowly out of the trees. Emmaline helped him to his feet, and he left the group to approach Sertus.

"Sertus, anything to report?" He braced himself for another slew of bad news and the grip of panic that had a near-constant hold on his heart.

Sertus shook his head. "We seem to be all clear for now. We're a bit farther north than the king's men usually go. Of course, that could change any day. I think he's getting more desperate. He knows we survive; he just doesn't know how or where. We'll have to wait and see what Avareck says when he returns. He went to scout out the southern tribes, didn't he?"

Rafayel shook his head in frustration. The southern tribes had declined his offer for the map of hiding places and instead chose to try to live as they had before this calamity began. "I warned him not to. It's too dangerous and too close to the castle. But you know him. He's young and foolish. Always has to try to prove himself. So *if* he happens to return, we'll hear what he has to report. Of course, we'll have to get to him before his mother does." He chuckled softly and clapped his old friend on the back. "Thank you, Sertus. I know it's difficult to be away from your family. Please, eat and warm yourself by the fire. Just don't get too comfortable. We're leaving first thing tomorrow morning."

Sertus nodded respectfully to his chief and headed toward his waiting family.

Once again, Rafayel smiled sadly as he watched the scout embrace his wife and three children. Others had been able to protect those they loved from the attacks. Why hadn't he?

The chief was so wrapped up in his own thoughts that he jumped when he heard a cry of alarm from Mytra Melkendra, whose son Avareck was approaching them from the opposite side of the camp.

"Where HAVE you been?" she yelled, storming towards him at a furious pace.

The young man flinched as his frantic mother grabbed him by the ear.

"Do you realize we've all been worried sick? Never mind that your father and I warned you, but the chief himself *forbade* you from going to the southern tribes! What do you do? You go anyway! Of all the stupid, insolent things to do for your pride, boy..." Mytra continued berating her son as he tried in vain to explain himself.

Rafayel was angry with the young scout as well, but there was no need for the noise and attention that could be drawn by the woman's volume and harsh words. He quickly made his way over to them and put a hand on her shoulder. "Mytra," he said calmly. She turned sharply and softened her expression as the chief continued. "We are targets in a war zone. It's best not to draw attention to ourselves with unnecessary noise. I need to hear Avareck's report, then you may continue your lecture *quietly*." He pursed his lips and motioned for her to let the boy go.

Mytra growled deep in her throat, glared at her son, and roughly released him from her grip. "We're not finished, Avareck Melkendra." She stalked off in a huff, muttering to herself.

"Sorry, Mum." Avareck sourly watched her walk away as he rubbed his sore ear.

The chief looked at him sternly, then gestured in Mytra's direction. "She does have a point, you know. What you did was reckless and dangerous."

Avareck kneeled, hanging his head soberly, and the chief softened his tone. "Avareck, I don't understand why you insist on taking these risks. You are strong and capable. That's why I made you a scout in the first place. We need you to help keep us safe. But I can't have you risking the tribe for your ego. You're better than that. And you're only twenty. Your life should be worth more than your pride."

Avareck raised his head and gave the older man a contrite look as he rose from his knees.

Rafayel grasped his shoulder and looked him square in the eyes. "You know you were once meant to be chief alongside my daughter. You also know I can no longer guarantee that will happen since she's gone." He paused as Avareck's face hardened. This was a sore topic, but it had to be discussed. "I'm sorry that your future is uncertain, son. Your dilemma has not escaped my notice, trust me. But I can't do anything to help that if you refuse to be responsible. Furthermore, these people need to know that their welfare is more important than their leader's impulses. You need to be willing to put them first, understand?"

Avareck nodded, his jaw still clenched.

"Next time I give you an order, please do not disobey me," the chief concluded his lecture. Sometimes, being chief meant having tough conversations and making difficult decisions. The boy would have to learn that if he wanted to be a leader.

"Now." Rafayel resumed his chiefly demeanor. "Since you *did* risk all our lives to go to the southern tribes, did you happen to pick up any useful information?"

Avareck's voice held a hint of indignance, but he spoke respectfully. "Well, my chief, the king appears to be increasing the number of raiding parties to try to find us. Although he still has yet to enter a battle himself."

The chief rolled his eyes. King Steflan was a coward. Even his armies knew it. He turned to walk towards his wagon and motioned for Avareck to follow. "That's not new information, boy. Do you have anything even remotely helpful?"

Even with his two good legs, Avareck struggled to keep up with the chief. He, along with most of the tribe, often wondered why Rafayel bothered using a crutch. He seemed able to walk perfectly fine on his own. "Well, sir, there's been a bit of an upset to the king's plans. I've heard much talk of a rogue warrior. They call her the Huntress. Rumor has it that she's one of us. She and her companion have been ambushing the king's soldiers. Somehow, the two of them stopped the raiders right in their path! They've saved a lot of people and are gaining a lot of trust and support."

Rafayel scoffed and pulled his ledgers out of a trunk. "She won't last long. None of them do."

Avareck pressed on excitedly. "But she's gotten other tribes talking of fighting back! No one has ever been able to get people's hopes up like that. Maybe she could be the one who finally stops all this."

The chief shook his head and waved Avareck away. "Your mother wanted to speak with you. Let's not keep her waiting any longer. Thank you for the information." He was not about to get his hopes up. This "Huntress," with her ambushes and talk of freedom, could be very influential, especially to the younger generations. Those dreams, however, would be short-lived. He remembered others who had tried. Where had that gotten them? Nowhere but a swift trip to the gallows. The Havani were not a race of warriors. They'd never had to be. At least, not before. Their attempts to protect themselves from attack were often futile. Two so-called "warriors" were no match for the king's soldiers, especially young and foolish warriors, as these likely were. No, it would be best for everyone if they just lived with the expectation that they could never again exist without hiding and that any day had the potential to be their last.

Chapter Eight

"Thank you, my dear cousin, for allowing us to visit last month. The children enjoyed it immensely. They never seem to be bored with just me for company, but it's nice for them to have the chance to spend time with others their own age. Yes, they are indeed growing up fast! In a few years, they will be adults, although I still remember taking them in like it was yesterday. Their skills are becoming quite impressive as well. Xanya has told me on many occasions that all she wants is to save her people from that murderous tyrant on the throne. I believe she can do it. But I fear I won't live to see it for myself..."

-Personal letter from Balthazar to a relative

Many miles away, on the outskirts of a small village, the young Havani woman now known as the Huntress removed her black hood and regarded the wanted poster displaying her assumed likeness. Her violet eyes sparkled as she smiled proudly and turned to face the young man behind her.

"So what do you make of this nickname they've given you?" The young man gently shoved the girl in the arm.

"I like it." She pulled her shoulders back and said in a mock regal tone, "I am the Huntress. Fear me." She laughed out loud. "What do you think, Dom?"

Dominic grinned back. "Well, it certainly fits you, Xanya Fortista. And when they finally get me up there, they can call me your shadow."

Xanya playfully narrowed her eyes at her friend. "C'mon, you know you're much more to me than that. I couldn't do any of this without you." She turned back to the poster, placing her hands on her narrow hips. "Good thing they can't seem to get my face right, though."

Dominic nodded in agreement. The portrait on the poster was too old. Too rough, wild, and angry-looking. Xanya's small stature, violet eyes, Havani porcelain skin, and raven hair gave her a uniquely striking appearance, nothing like one would expect of her growing reputation. Whoever was drawing these posters obviously could not imagine such a great warrior could be so young and beautiful. Much to her credit, Xanya never thought of herself in such shallow terms. She barely stood to his shoulder, but she intimidated Dominic more than anyone he had ever known, including Balthazar. She was confident, fearless, and compassionate. If anyone could save the Havani from the wrath of King Steflan, it would be her.

Dominic tugged affectionately on Xayna's ebony braid, as he always did when teasing her. "C'mon Huntress, you'd better get out of here before someone spots you. We still need supplies. How much money have we got?"

Xanya reached for a small coin pouch at her waist and tossed it to him. "Try not to use all of it."

"Only if you promise to stay hidden," he warned. "Now go." He pointed authoritatively towards the woods.

"Yeah, yeah, I'm going," she said snarkily as she turned to leave. "But you still can't tell me what to do!"

"I wouldn't even dare try." Dominic smiled and watched her disappear into the trees before heading towards town.

Tossing the clinking bag of coins in his hand, Dominic made his way to the small village of Hobdaiy, about half a mile from the forest's edge. Hobdaiy wasn't much to look at, but it was rather well known for being the "last stop"; the last bit of civilization before entering the heart of Enderhail's vast wilderness. If one wished to venture further, it would be foolish not to stop and replenish supplies here. Despite its diminutive appearance, its location and reputation made the village a rather thriving hub.

Dom hoped he wouldn't have to spend all their money. He'd figured they didn't have much, but tossing the bag around made him realize just how low they were on funds. Their vigilante activities left precious little time for the trapping business Balthazar had so diligently passed on to them.

The soldiers patrolling the perimeter paid him no mind as he passed them and continued into the heart of town. To them, he was just another lonely traveler. He wanted to keep it that way. Xanya never accompanied him on these occasional supply trips; her prominent Havani features would attract too much attention. Balthazar had done the same with their own nearby town of Baernside when they were children, so Xanya had never set foot in even a small village such as this. These sights and sounds would all be a marvel to her.

The dusty roads wound around small shops and stalls, dilapidated buildings, and vendors calling out their wares to passersby. Dominic breathed in the scent of burning fires, hot food, tar, and the general stench of people and animals being forced to live in a shared space. He preferred the smell of the woods, the trees and soil, the running rivers and streams, and the occasional burning of fires rather than the constant scorching of stoves.

The street stalls were tempting, with their unique smells and the colorful sorts of people who seemed to run them. This, however, needed to be a quick trip, so he made his way to the large shop in the very center of the clustered buildings. That was his strategy whenever he had to go to town: get in, get out, get back. He wasn't the least bit worried about Xanya. She was more than capable of taking care of herself. He just felt more like himself in the forest.

A group of young women stared as he walked by, and he gave them a polite nod and small smile. He shook his head as his admirers shuffled away, giggling and whispering to one another. Dominic had grown into a fine young man: medium height but well built, with warm brown eyes and slightly wavy brown hair that usually fell into his eyes. He often got attention like that in the villages, but those girls always seemed so frivolous and simple to him. They just couldn't measure up to the girl he already had. Or wanted, rather. He'd never dared to even bring up the subject. Maybe someday he would.

Dom finally reached the shop and smiled as he was enveloped by the warmth of the indoors. The woods had given him and Xanya a good life. Still, he sometimes wondered what it would be like to live the way these people did, with everyday work and a comfortable home. The shop was large and cozy, with a fireplace in one corner and its walls lined with shelves housing many items he recognized and some he did not. *I could run a shop like this. Seems like a nice way to live.*

Lost in his daydreams, the young man didn't notice the shopkeeper come up from the cellar.

"Can I 'elp you with somethin', son?"

Dominic jumped and turned to approach the portly older man behind the counter. "Yes, sir, I'm sorry. I was just admiring your selection."

The man smiled and gave a nod of gratitude. "My wife and I 'ave spent many years buildin' our life and business' ere. We're very 'appy 'elpin' travelers like yerrself. What can I get for ye?"

Dominic spilled the coins out onto the counter and listed what he needed. As the shopkeeper took the money and gathered the requested items, Dominic glanced at another Huntress WANTED poster on the wall. This one had been done by a different artist, but it was just as inaccurate as the one they'd seen outside town. He choked down a laugh.

The shopkeeper followed his gaze. "I only put those up 'cause the guards make me. You know, a lot of us 'round these parts don't like what the king is doin'. Those nomads are good people. They mind their own business and 'elp others when they can. Can't imagine why the king would be after 'em. Whoever this 'untress is, she's doing good work. She's not likely an ordinary warrior, is she, lad?"

Dominic tried to hide his smile. "No sir, I don't believe she is." He looked up at the shelves behind the counter and spotted a jar of Xanya's favorite candies. He and Balthazar never liked leaving Xanya behind whenever they went to a village and always brought her a little gift for their return. Since the untimely death of their beloved guardian, Dominic had kept up the tradition on his own. He counted out the coins he had left on the counter and handed the older man half of them, pointing to the jar. "Will this cover some of those?"

The shopkeeper smiled and poured some of the candy into another small pouch, which Dom tossed into his pack with the rest of his purchase. He thanked the shopkeeper for his services and took his leave, quickly returning through town towards the familiar shadow of the woods.

The morning hours had just barely passed away, and gray clouds were starting to roll in. Whatever the weather, Dominic and Xanya would most likely spend the rest of the day scouting for the king's troops or trying to contact lingering Havani tribes. Sadly, some family lines had been wiped out completely. But by the pair's calculations, there were still several hundred of the nomads living in tribes scattered throughout the kingdom. Dom thought she was mad for even thinking of it, but if Xanya was serious about her developing plan, they would need every willing Havani they could find.

Passing through the first line of trees gave the young man a sense of comfort and welcome. That morning was not the first time he'd entertained thoughts of living in a village and having what some would consider a more "normal" life. But those desires always disappeared the moment he came back to the woods. Dominic might never know where he had come from, but he knew this was where he belonged.

He walked through the trees for about half an hour and climbed a small ridge before their camp came into view.

Xanya looked up from two rabbits roasting on the fire and smiled brightly. "You hungry?"

The day had been a productive one. They hadn't come upon any of the king's troops, a rare occurrence that was both a relief and a cause for concern. They wondered if perhaps the king was biding his time, reserving his troops to plan something big. Whatever the reason, there was nothing else they could do for the time being, and they had retreated back to their camp for a warm fire and supper of perfectly roasted venison.

Xanya had been delighted with both the candies and the fact that Dominic hadn't spent all of their money. "Just most of it," he'd replied with a wink when she'd asked.

While Xanya busied herself with tending to the horses, Dom sat on a fallen tree trunk near the fire and pulled out his whittling. Balthazar had been quick to pass all his skills onto them, including the ones he reserved for evenings by the fire.

"I ran into a scout from Chief Grogan's tribe while you were gone today. Arden, his name was." Xanya paused in brushing her mount to share the information.

Dominic looked up abruptly. "Really? I thought they were all but wiped out in the last raid! What happened?"

"Well, first, I apologized that we weren't in the area to help at the time," Xanya said sheepishly.

"Xanya," Dominic gently chastised her. "Nothing that happens is our fault. You know that. This kingdom is massive! At any given time, we could be several days' ride from any of the tribes. We can't be in every corner of the forest at once."

"I know," she replied sadly. "But I felt like I had to say something. Anyway, Arden mentioned that a handful of them survived and joined another tribe under Chief Cadoc's rule. I've never met him myself, but Arden said Grogan's story of us helping others has inspired them. They actually fought off some of the king's men all on their own!"

Dominic beamed at her and pointed with his knife. "How many times have I told you that you inspire people? There's some proof for you right there. Don't ever doubt what you've done."

Xanya's embarrassed grin made Dom's heart skip a beat as she returned attention to her horse. He pressed his knife back to the wood, hoping he didn't look as red as he felt.

Several long minutes passed as they worked in contented silence. Out of the corner of his eye, Dominic finally caught Xanya's gaze fixated on him, and he smiled as he continued his work. "I can see you staring at me, Xanya. I know what that look means. What's on your mind?"

She folded her arms, and her expression became quizzical. "Do you ever wonder where you came from?"

Dominic chuckled. "You've asked me that before, you know, and it's always the same answer. All I remember is my mother singing to me. I don't remember what she looked like or the song. Just that it happened." His head began to hurt at the wisp of a memory, as if his brain was reaching for something just out of its grasp. This happened occasionally; the rare times he corrected Xanya's technique when sparring or shared an insight on how to diplomatically deal with certain tribes. *"How do you know that?"* She would always ask. He could never tell her. This was knowledge he simply shouldn't have. Sometimes it terrified him.

Xanya gave him an exasperated sigh, obviously trying to stifle a laugh. "Yes, I know that. But I'm serious, and you didn't answer my question. Do you ever really wonder where you came from? Who you might be if you hadn't lost your memory?"

He set down his carving and stared into the crackling fire, tugging on the tattered blue scarf tied around his neck. The remains of his childhood blanket were all he had of his former life. "Do you remember the first few months I was with you, and Balthazar tried to find my family whenever he took me into town? He would ask around to see if anyone had heard about a missing boy. I was always terrified he was really going to find my parents."

Xanya gave him a sad smile. "I was always terrified he might come back without you."

Once Balthazar heard of the escalating situation with the Havani, he decided it would be safer for Xanya to stay with him rather than try to get her back to her tribe. He eventually also gave up on finding Dom's family after months without success. The children were thrilled when they learned they would no longer have to live in fear of separation.

Dominic continued. "If he had found them, I would have had to go back to being whoever or whatever boring thing I probably was before. Honestly, I would have taken the first opportunity to run back to the woods and find you. No matter what my life was before, I think you two were meant to be my real family."

He pushed the hair out of his eyes and blinked away the growing tears. It wasn't the dreams of battles, blood, and death that kept him up at night. It was the nightmare where he woke up being someone else, without Xanya, without Balthazar, without being able to help save innocent lives and fight for what was right. He looked up at his friend, her face glowing in the flames of their campfire. "I don't need or want to know who or what I was. I like who I am."

"We were both lucky to have him, weren't we?" Xanya's voice cracked. Dominic nodded silently as she came and sat next to him.

Balthazar's death had been sudden, though he'd been sick for quite a while. Despite everything they'd accomplished since, these past six months without him had been jarring. He had seemed indestructible. Every once in a while, they still expected to hear his booming laugh, a kind word, or gentle correction in whatever they were doing. The absence of his larger-than-life presence had left their world feeling empty and vast. They'd realized they needed to grow up fast. And that they needed each other now more than ever. It wasn't just the Havani they fought for; it was the memory of the man who raised them and the principles he believed in. With any luck, he would be proud of what they were doing. Worried, surely, but hopefully also proud.

It wasn't long before their conversation trailed off, and Xanya's head slumped against Dominic's shoulder. He smiled and carefully moved the sleeping girl to a pile of fallen leaves on the ground, covering her with one of Balthazar's heavy pelts they carried with them. He grabbed another and wrapped it around his shoulders, positioning himself with his sword on his lap and the best view of the surrounding landscape. He was happy to take the first watch that night.

Chapter Nine

"*Blood is shed, but lives are saved in the wake of the Huntress.*"

-Verse from a new Havani song

Xanya and Dominic peeked their heads over the ridge of a small waterfall and observed the soldiers passing below. The clear water sparkled and tumbled over into the river, offering the perfect cover for the pair of young spies. Xanya's eyes darted around the crowd, taking a mental inventory of the group's weapons and other tools. *No more than twenty men of various ages, only two archers, should give us good odds. They all look half-drunk, anyhow.* She raised her face skyward and noted the sun's position, only partially covered by clouds. *It's a little early for that.* She turned her gaze back to the pitiful scene before her.

This rag-tag group of men was clearly not composed of trained soldiers but of villagers who had volunteered solely for the modest profit the king had promised for their services. Though their armor was imprinted with the royal seal on the right shoulder, their behavior was undisciplined, uncouth, and unfocused. Watching them in action would be...interesting, at the very least.

Xanya didn't know how involved the king was with the day-to-day operation of the atrocities he carried out against her people. He would, no doubt, be thoroughly disappointed with this particular bunch. For a brief moment, she almost found herself feeling sorry for them. They were either in desperate situations or downright vile men to have willingly volunteered for such a horrible task. Either way, she didn't wish their obvious misery on anyone.

"Xanya, they're right there," Dom whispered. "Most of them look like they've already had too much ale. They're easy targets. Why don't we just stop them now, before they can do any harm?"

"That's the point." She offered him a stern side glance. "They haven't done *anything* yet. What if they're just a scouting party?"

"An armed scouting party? Of twenty men?" Her friend's tone was more than skeptical.

"We're not cold-blooded killers, Dom. We don't attack until they do." Xanya rose from her crouching position as the band moved out of view and started after them.

Dominic gave a disgruntled mumble and followed, watching the ground for clear places to step. This "rule" of hers was one of the few things they disagreed on. He understood her line of logic: they didn't want to be guilty of the same crimes as the king's men, attacking innocent victims. But if they *knew* what they were going to do and could stop them ahead of time, couldn't they save more lives? However, this point was important to her, so he rarely expressed his reservations.

Xanya continued leading the way, trailing behind the troops and ensuring they were undetected. If the poor louts had bothered to glance behind, they would have seen the two young warriors sneaking up on them, weapons at the ready.

They followed the men for about an hour, with the sun eventually disappearing behind the clouds and giving way to a steady drizzle of rain. The soldiers were not at all concerned with keeping their presence a secret and began to complain loudly about getting wet. Hidden behind two large trees, Xanya caught Dominic's smirk and pointedly rolled her eyes. *Sorcerers, we live out here, you oafs, and we LIKE it. A little water shouldn't bother the brave soldiers of the mighty King Steflan.*

The soldiers suddenly stopped and crouched, gesturing in hushed tones and checking their weapons. *They've found a tribe.* Xanya signaled to Dominic. She saw his body tense as he tightened his scabbard belt, pulled up his hood, and put his scarf over his face. He always got nervous right before a fight. Their chain mail-lined leather armor offered plenty of protection, but there was still a chance the worst could happen. Neither one of them wanted that, but they also knew they were both willing to give their lives if necessary.

Xanya gave her friend a reassuring smile and a wink before pulling up her own hood and face covering. She peeked around the tree again.

The soldiers had begun to disperse, most likely spreading themselves around the perimeter of the encampment to maximize their element of surprise. The only ones who stayed put were the two archers, who would have a good vantage point at the top of the hill. Xanya could easily take care of them.

The men rushed into action with a battle cry, which was quickly drowned out by the screams of the terrified Havani.

Xanya nocked an arrow and expertly downed one of the archers. As his comrade turned in surprise, she finally stepped out from her hiding spot and hit him square in the chest. His eyes widened as he fell backward into the fray, leaving the hill available for Xanya to scan the battle, arrows flying from her bow.

Dominic took off and immediately jumped into the chaos, cutting a soldier off from his lunge toward a young boy who was bravely brandishing a wooden sword. "Run!" He ordered the child as he blocked a blow and punched the larger man in the jaw. His foe momentarily dazed, Dom's sword found a gap in his armor and stabbed, bringing his opponent to his knees with a cry of pain. He kicked the soldier in the head and turned to face the next man who dared attack him.

The king's men were more aggressive than anticipated. However, their lack of proper training and technique gave them a stark disadvantage against their enemies.

From her vantage point above the battle, Xanya noticed the Havani had gathered their meager weapons and were bravely holding them off. She was more than impressed with their efforts.

A sense of dread came over her as she prepared to lose another arrow. Anyone watching would have noticed her eyes flash under her hood as she turned to see one of the soldiers sneaking up on her. She'd been found. She ran at the man and smacked him cleanly in the face with her bow, then stabbed him in the side with an arrow. Leaving the soldier lying on the ground, she hurried over the crest of the hill and jumped into the battle, strapping her bow to her back and drawing her trusty old sword as she did so.

Dominic smiled as he saw his friend add her blade to the fray. Xanya was an incredible archer, and her arrows never missed. At the same time, it was amazing to watch her fight with a sword. She was always so *fast*. No matter how many times they sparred, she was constantly one step ahead of him. It was the same with her enemies. They never saw her coming until it was too late. There was always a certain sparkle in her violet eyes when she fought. Not from any pleasure she took in ending lives but from the ferocity and determination of a woman who knew she fought for justice and peace.

It wasn't long before only seven of the king's men were left, and they quickly took off into the woods. They had known they were outnumbered before the attack, but they hadn't counted on the Havani fighting back. Nor had they counted on the Huntress. The king would not be pleased with the report they brought back, but at least they would still get paid. They hoped.

Xanya stood heavy-hearted, counting the bodies that littered the forest floor. There were far more Havani corpses than she would have liked, but at least they managed to save most of the tribe. As if that fact was helpful to the dead and their families. But there was no time to dwell. Once again, she would have to bury her grief and rage deep within, just as they would bury the remains of those she had failed to save.

Dominic was giving instructions to those nearest to them. "Separate your dead from the soldiers and bury them properly. We'll dig a mass grave for the king's men. You can't stay here long, but we'll do what we can to help." He turned to Xanya, "Shall I go and find the chief for you?"

As the Huntress raised her head to reply, her eyes found the face of a busy young man in the crowd, one who was undeniably familiar. She furrowed her brows and racked her brain, digging into the recesses of her memory for a name. *Avareck? How did...* She slowly turned her gaze to the other people milling about and almost stopped breathing as she recognized practically every single one. These faces, nearly forgotten, were now right before her eyes, forlorn and ragged but full of spirit. Names returned to her slowly, and she fought the urge to cry out to each of them. She grasped Dominic's shoulder for support as her knees buckled.

He grabbed her waist to steady her and pulled down his scarf, searching her face with concern. "Xanya, what's wrong?"

Her voice shook as she spoke. "Dom...I think this is *my* tribe."

His eyes widened in surprise as he looked around. "Are you sure?"

"Yes, I'm sure. I know most of these people. I can name ten of them right in front of us. We've found my family." She finally let out her bated breath and hugged him tightly, a strange combination of relief and terror coming over her. "I don't know if I can force myself to stay hidden when I know these are my people. You'll help me, right? We have to keep our identities a secret. That's a risk we can't take."

Dominic nodded and replaced his scarf as she pulled away from his embrace. "You know I'm here for you, always. Let's see if we can find the chief."

Before they could even begin to search for someone who looked to be in charge, a woman confidently strode up to them and crossed her arms. She immediately launched into what could have been mistaken for a prepared dialogue. "You are the one known as the Huntress, are you not?"

Xanya swallowed a gasp as she recognized her cousin's face, though older and more worn than she remembered. *Oh, Emmaline, I've missed you.* "Yes, I am." She tried to appear confident as she answered. "My companion and I would like to speak with your chief. We are here to help you."

Emmaline's expression softened at the sound of the Huntress' youthful voice. "We thank you for your courage and service, both of you. But I do not believe my uncle would wish to speak to you. He does not approve of your actions."

The blood drained from Xanya's face, and she swallowed hard. "Your uncle?"

"Yes. I am his only living relative, and I help to lead this tribe. He feels you will only destroy yourself with this foolish undertaking. Although I must admit, you've accomplished much more than any previous rebels have." A slight admiration crept into Emmaline's voice, forcing Xanya to hold back a smile under her face covering.

"I appreciate your uncle's reservations, but we are only trying to do our part to save the Havani. We *must* see him immediately," Xanya insisted.

Emmaline shook her head. "Well, you're a determined little thing, I'll give you that. I can take you to him, but I must warn you that he has very little patience these days." She beckoned. "Come with me."

They followed Emmaline through the crowd, pointedly ignoring the whispers and stares of the tribal onlookers. Rumors of these two warriors had been circulating the kingdom for months, but none from this tribe had yet encountered them in person. Xanya wondered what they would say now if they knew her identity.

The trio stopped in front of the largest tent in the camp, and Emmaline gestured for Xanya and Dominic to stay outside. She entered, and the two visitors heard a hushed, frustrated conversation coming from the structure. Xanya couldn't stop herself from shaking, but she stayed silent so as to not alarm Dominic. *All these years, I thought he was dead, and now...*

Emmaline reappeared at the tent flap. "He'll speak with you alone, Huntress. Your man and I will see to the burials." She led Dominic away before either of them could protest.

Xanya hated the idea of doing this without him. Talking to the chiefs was a particular talent of his for reasons neither of them could work out. If this chief was who she thought he was, she would need Dom more than ever. She supposed she had no choice. After a few moments, she took a deep, shaky breath, prayed silently to the Sorcerers, and entered the tent.

Sitting on a stump surrounded by pieces of parchment was her father, Chief Rafayel Fortista. He was older and more frail than she remembered, and his hair had begun to gray. He didn't even raise his head to acknowledge her. But it was certainly him, and he was very much alive.

Xanya had no idea how she was going to get through this. All she wanted was to run to him, to tell him everything she'd been doing and learning for the last ten years. To be there for him as a daughter should. She had to keep herself at bay. *Just open your mouth and speak. You never have trouble with that.*

She cleared her throat and began, "Chief Fortista, I am–"

"I know who you are," his deep voice cut her off abruptly. He kept his face buried in the parchment he was scrawling on, using a short wooden stool as a table.

He was never good at hiding his emotions. And he's not happy with me. "Then you know why I'm here. The injustices perpetrated by King Steflan have been going on for ten years too long. It's time we did something about them. The Havani is a strong and noble race. We have the power to fight back. We need only to join forces and strike together."

The chief paused in his scribbling and finally looked up at her. His face had aged far more than the decade that had passed since she last saw him. However, underneath it all, he was still the handsome and intimidating man who had raised her for the first eight years of her life. She gasped silently as he struggled to get up and reached for his crutch. Like Balthazar, he'd seemed indestructible. That is until the day she thought she saw him die.

Her father hobbled toward her, eyeing the tiny figure before him, and shook his head. "What do you intend to do, child? Raise a Havani army and go to war with the king?"

She squared her shoulders and stood as tall as she could. "That is exactly what I intend to do, sir."

The chief blinked and then, to Xanya's surprise, laughed out loud. "Your confidence is foolhardy, girl. Do you think you're the first one to try to fight this? The first one who's survived this long? I've seen many like you who thought they could make a difference. They were all killed, and you will be, too. Just as all of us eventually will be."

Rafayel's face fell, and his laughter ceased, his tone becoming soft and vulnerable. "My world shattered ten years ago. They took my daughter from me. I didn't even get to bury her. So don't you dare stand there and give me false hope for the future! We have no future. Furthermore, I refuse to align myself with someone I can't trust and will not trust someone who refuses to show me their face. So if you'll excuse me–"

Xanya couldn't bear it for a second longer. With tears pouring down her cheeks, she ripped off her hood and face covering and looked him straight in the eyes. "Papa."

Chief Fortista stopped breathing and dropped his crutch, stumbling to the ground as his daughter ran to him. She wrapped her arms around his neck and held him as tightly as she could, never wanting to let go as long as she lived. She could feel his heart pounding in his chest as he sobbed into her shoulder, incomprehensible words spilling from his lips. After several minutes, the chief pulled away and grasped her face, taking in all her features before resting his forehead against hers. Neither of them could believe it, but they were alive and together, a family once more.

The day had taken quite a surprising turn. After what felt like hours, Xanya and the chief burst from the tent, declaring the good news for the entire crowd.

"My daughter has returned!" Rafayel's voice had boomed through the tribe.

After the initial bout of shock wore off, Dominic could barely contain his happiness for his friend. He never thought he'd get to meet anyone from Xanya's tribe, least of all her father, whom she'd thought to be dead all these years. He'd been built up as something of a legend in Dominic's mind. It was incredible to see the man alive and well.

When Xanya finally broke away from the crowd that had gathered around her, Dominic gave her a mischievous smile and raised one eyebrow. "What happened to keeping our identities a secret?"

"I know, I know, I'm sorry. I tried, I really did! I just..." she met his eyes and finally broke, the tears welling up again. "He was right there in front of me, Dom, after all these years. Telling me about his daughter who'd been killed," she stuttered. "I never, in my wildest dreams, thought he could be alive, just as he probably felt about me. How could I stand there and let him continue to grieve when I had the opportunity to speak up and heal us both?"

In a single moment of unabashed confidence, Dominic gently wiped the tears from her face with his thumb, leaving his hand on her cheek. "Xanya, you don't have to explain anything to me." Suddenly embarrassed, he moved the hand to her shoulder and felt his heart pound as she covered it with her own. "But I can't help but wonder if this could only improve our situation." He glanced around the bustling tribe.

"Yes," she replied slowly, following his eyes around the camp and turning to meet his winsome smile. "Yes, we can always ride out from wherever we are to help other tribes..."

"Maybe even tempt some recruits to help us if your father will allow it." Dominic grinned again, released Xanya's shoulder, and headed towards the middle of the camp, leaving the young woman beaming behind him. Staying here wouldn't have to mean giving up their mission. They couldn't do that. On the other hand, it could provide them a new vantage point from which to attack their formidable enemies: hiding in plain sight amongst the very people being hunted. The fact that this particular tribe was Xanya's own family was just a bonus.

It seemed strange to have something to celebrate on a day when they'd lost so many of their kin, but Chief Fortista felt they needed to welcome his daughter home properly. After gathering for the burial rites and ceremonies, food and drink were prepared and distributed, and the tribe sat in commiseration and celebration. The usual music and dancing were, of course, out of the question, but that didn't matter. The relaxation of the company after such a terrible morning was a welcome distraction.

Dominic sat on a rock near one of the large fires, chortling into his cup of cider while Emmaline regaled him and a few others with stories of little Xanya. He almost wished they'd been younger when they met so he could have seen the sillier, more rambunctious side of the girl he knew.

Emmaline wiped happy tears from her eyes as she concluded the story of four-year-old Xanya dumping all her father's clothes in the nearby river to be washed, unaware they would flow downstream. "It took four men over an hour to fish them all out! All she could say for herself was, 'Well Papa, they got clean, didn't they?'" Emmaline shook her head in the chorus of laughter and got up to get more food.

Dominic found his eyes scanning the camp, observing the faces of all present and trying to remember those he'd met. He finally made eye contact with Xanya and started to raise his hand in a wave. His stomach tightened as he noticed who she was talking to. Avareck Melkendra had been annoyingly hovering over her like a bee over a flower since her identity had been revealed. Dom knew precisely why he felt the way he did, but there was something else about the other young man he didn't like.

Emmaline returned with a full plate and didn't hesitate to dig in. Dominic leaned towards her slightly, keeping his eyes on Xanya and Avareck. "So, what's Avareck's story? Did he and Xanya know each other well?"

Emmaline looked up from her meal, followed Dominic's gaze, and then turned to him sympathetically. "They were friends as children," she confirmed between bites. "Of course, all children who grow up together tend to be friends until they reach a certain age. I don't know if they would have gotten along once they grew up. It's probably a good thing her father called off their betrothal, for their sakes and the tribe's."

Dominic almost choked on his drink and met the woman's eyes. "Betrothal?"

Emmaline blushed at her gaffe and pursed her lips, swallowing a mouthful. "Sorry, I wasn't supposed to mention that. Uncle didn't want to burden her with it so soon after her return. Well, it's all moot now anyway." She gave him a knowing look before turning back to her food.

Dom warily looked back to Xanya and Avareck, his heart sinking as they went in to hug one another. His disappointment turned to anger when Avereck found his stare and gave him a sneer over Xanya's shoulder. Dominic glowered back, refusing to break eye contact as the two pulled apart.

Unaware of the staring contest going on behind her, Xanya awkwardly broke from her childhood friend's embrace and gave him a closed-lipped smile. Avareck had clearly been eager to speak with her, though they had very little to talk about. The man before her now was virtually a stranger.

"It's good to have you home, Xanya." Avareck squeezed her shoulder as he took his leave. "I hope we can speak again in the near future."

"I'm sure we will," she answered dryly. *I hope he doesn't think I'm still obligated to marry him. Papa wouldn't hold me to that after all these years.*

Xanya returned a few kind greetings as she gazed through the crowd, then grinned widely as she spotted Dominic and hurried over to wrap him in a real hug, the kind she could never give the man who'd just left her side.

Dom relaxed in her warm embrace. "I'm happy for you," he said as she released him. "Your family is all here. I suppose that means I can go now?" He stuck his thumb over his shoulder with a cheeky expression.

Xanya punched him lightly in the arm as he chuckled at his own joke. "Don't think you can get away from me that easily, Dom. As far as I'm concerned, you're stuck."

"Fine, have it your way, princess. You might one day regret those words." He stuck his tongue out at her as she backed away from him mischievously. Dominic wasn't really sure how he would describe their relationship, but he would never consider himself "stuck." Not when it came to her.

As the festive air began to fade, scouts were sent out to retrieve Xanya and Dominic's horses so they could join in the trek to the next campsite. Rafayel had humbly shown them the map that described the series of numerous caves, hollows, and thickets that he had compiled as a network of hiding places for their people. Xanya and Dominic had no idea how this arrangement had escaped their knowledge thus far, but it was now apparent how so many of the Havani had survived for so long. It was anyone's guess why some of the chiefs had refused the life-saving information.

The tribe traveled slowly but with purpose, eager to get to their next destination. Some respites were further apart than others, but this one was no more than a day's travel. Xanya rode between her father and cousin, talking and laughing, with a smile on her face that Dominic felt he'd never truly seen until today. She was entirely and purely happy. That was all he'd ever wanted for her. He felt privileged to be there to witness it.

He'd been tasked with scouting ahead with some other young men and had reluctantly ridden away from the joyous scene. However, he was glad to have time alone to gather his thoughts. It was amazing how completely one's life could change in an afternoon.

As Dom scanned the area through the trees, Avereck rode up beside him. They'd briefly conversed while packing up, and everything about the young Havani man rubbed him the wrong way, not just the attention he'd been giving Xanya.

"So it must have been great growing up with Xanya, huh? She would be the best sister," Avareck said. An insincere grin spread across his face.

Dom groaned internally. He was determined not to give Avareck the satisfaction of getting under his skin. "I never thought of Xanya as a sister," he said matter of factly. "And I don't think she's ever thought of me as a brother. Balthazar never treated us that way."

Avareck furrowed his brows. "Well, all I'm saying is that being raised together as you were creates a different kind of bond. One that may not necessarily change."

"All Xanya wants is to save her people, and I am standing beside her."

"So what if you do accomplish that goal?" Avareck goaded him on. "What happens to the two of you after that?"

Dominic turned his horse, cutting Averek off from his path. If they were going to do this, he wanted it to be on his terms. "Look, Melkendra, if you have something to say to me, you're going to have to be a little more direct."

Avareck scowled. "You want me to be direct? Fine. I'll spell it out for you. When we were children, Xanya was betrothed to me. Now that she has returned, I believe that agreement should still stand."

Though taken aback by his boldness, Dominic scoffed confidently. "She's not that same little girl you knew, I can assure you. Don't you think she should be able to choose for herself? Or not at all? Besides, we're not sure we're staying that long." At least, he hoped they weren't *now*, given the confrontation he was being forced into. Maybe he could convince Xanya they needed to move on after all. *Could I really be selfish enough to ask her to leave her family again? Because of this childish lout?*

Avareck pointed at him exasperatedly. "Her father promised my family that I would marry her and be chief. I am the one who should lead us, with her by my side. I am the one who can give her a Havani heir. I've seen how you look at her, *lochrage,* and I can tell you right now that it's NOT going to happen." He again twisted his face into a small sneer.

Dominic's blood boiled as the slur reached his ears. Avareck had summoned up one of the few deliberately offensive terms that existed in his native tongue. *Lochrage* had never been used lightly, reserved as a descriptor for only the most vile of people who did not belong to the Havani race. Avareck was fortunate that none of the other members of the tribe had heard him use such a hateful term.

With a deep breath, Dominic maintained his outward calm, though he felt like decking the other man right off his horse. "We'll just have to cross that bridge when we come to it." He turned his mount to take his leave.

"I'll tell her," Avareck warned, smug now with the knowledge of his newfound rival's secret.

Dominic turned back to him sharply. "No, you won't," he growled. "Because if you do, you'll have to admit that you see her as nothing more than a prize to be won and shown off. I can promise you she won't like that at all." He kicked his horse and took off, leaving the Havani scout glaring daggers after him.

Chapter Ten

-Entry from the diary of Queen Alyssandra Felhold

Talis had once believed that the darkness eventually wouldn't bother him so much, and that one day he would learn to appreciate the cool stone, the rhythmic dripping sound from the ceiling, and the shadows from the flickering candlelight. Unfortunately, this hadn't been the case. Every day, he waited for the emptiness to dispel, for his soul to stop feeling so damp and clouded. That day never came. "Perhaps," he surmised to himself, as he often did now, "it never will."

As he stared around the dank, empty dungeon, he wondered when the others would arrive for the meeting. He looked to that time with a sense of both hope and dread. Hope, because he would no longer be alone, and dread because he would no longer be entirely himself.

Truthfully, he didn't think he could remember who he was. Not anymore.

Once again, he reached for the mirror he had requested from Kels and stared at his foreign reflection. Instead of his own face, that golden mask stared back like it had become part of his flesh. He had tried in vain to remove it like the others could, but Dormastis wanted him to be nothing more than a puppet. After all these years in the dungeon, Talis couldn't even remember what he looked like. He thought that was what terrified him most. "I chose this," he told himself casually as he returned the mirror to the small table at the side of his cot and stood. "That's all there is to it. I *chose* this."

Sometimes, he wished he hadn't. Sometimes, he wished he had turned his back on that inhuman monster when he still had the chance. To return to his family and friends, to the simple life he had so carelessly abandoned for the promise of power. A promise that, as of yet, had gone unfulfilled. Other times, that voice pulled on the back of his mind, the voice that had haunted him since the day he'd made his fateful choice. *The power will come. Patience.*

He wasn't sure if it was just in his mind or if someone was keeping him on the right path. The path that Dormastis had chosen for him, at least. Dormastis. That powerful sorcerer who had talked him into this cursed life. Or was it blessed? After so many centuries, he could no longer distinguish the difference.

Beginning to feel the shadow of doubt once again, Talis walked between the dripping candles on the floor and laid his long, bony fingers on the runes he'd painstakingly scratched into the wall. He traced them with his dirty nails and read the words aloud as he went. "Dormastis ruled, but now he sleeps. Forever in darkness, but never in peace. Peace is for those who get to die, not those whose souls are cast aside. Those tormented beings are now trapped beyond, suffering for deeds the world deemed wrong. They wait for their servants to succeed during their greatest time of need. For when they are ready to return, the world's rebirth will be justly earned."

The world's rebirth will be justly earned. Talis liked to think his own "rebirth" would be included in that victorious hour. Whenever it happened. Then, he would no longer be a lowly henchman but a powerful being in his own right. The doubts melted away as he traced the words over and over again. The phrases calmed his frayed nerves, and he drew in a breath. These periods of regret came from time to time. He'd slowly learned to push through them one at a time. They never did him any good anyway.

Renewed in his vigor, he turned back to the open room and went to kneel at the symbol of the flaming scythe that was etched into the floor. He stretched his mind beyond the confines of the dilapidated dungeon and the castle walls, searching, scanning the villages for those who might be sympathetic to their cause. Some would be brought to the castle for him to evaluate. Others, those with the strongest convictions, would simply be taken to the Outer Realm to live in the presence of their new master and learn of their grand scheme. *What a privilege!*

The trouble was, their plan was taking quite a bit longer than even he had anticipated, and Dormastis' patience was wearing thin. If they failed, Talis would undoubtedly take the blame. *I would deserve it, too.*

It wasn't long before he heard the scraping of stone on stone as one of his cohorts finally joined him in the gloom. He felt the familiar bout of anxiety as his own consciousness began to fade, making way for that of his master. There were days he fought this transition, days he didn't want to share control of his body and mind. Today was not one of them. He felt the strength fill his limbs, felt Dormastis' mind meld with his own. Even in his current weakened state, the ancient sorcerer possessed power greater than Talis had ever dreamed. His righteous fury and sweet satisfaction in his victims' pain now also belonged to his servant. And the servant relished them.

Lord Kels entered the room, pulling his silver mask over his face as he did so. Talis often thought the disguises were an unnecessary precaution. Each member knew of the others' identities anyway. But Dormastis had insisted on them on the grounds of both secrecy and tradition. He pointedly failed to share the significance of said tradition with his oldest and most loyal steward.

"Good morning, Lord Kels," Talis said, his voice not entirely his own. This was perhaps the strangest part of having his body used in such a way. It was an auditory reminder that he wasn't only himself in these moments; that someone else was there, too.

"Good morning." Kels gave a slight bow and offered Talis the tray he was carrying, full of the scraps he'd managed to sneak away from breakfast. Kels had been an obvious choice for their first contact inside the castle. As luck would have it, he was the last of Talis' family line and had always been obsessed with finding the missing links in his lineage. The middle-aged lord was terrified when Talis appeared in his chambers late one night to recruit him for the Scythe. Despite his initial misgivings, he eventually accepted Dormastis' offer of power and influence, just like his ancestor before him.

"Has the king shown any further signs of distress in your council meetings?" Talis nodded in thanks for the tray and fixed his dark eyes on the lord.

"Don't you know?" Kels inquired warily. He still wasn't sure he understood the arrangement between his ancestor and the sorcerer. Fear and reverence always seemed the best sentiments with which to approach these one-on-one interactions.

"My dear man, I know what Dormastis allows me to know. Nothing more." Talis often saw visions of events that were currently transpiring, both in the castle and the Outer Realm. But he was never granted the whole picture. The *why* behind the Scythe's actions wasn't always clear, even to their leader. Sometimes, Dormastis' orders even appeared to work in direct opposition to their goals. He dared not ask why. His master wished to keep certain things for himself. Dormastis knew everything in Talis' mind, but Talis saw only glimpses of his. The sorcerer alone was in control. It was not an arrangement for the faint of heart.

"Right." Kels cleared his throat. "The king does appear to be getting more and more disturbed. He's taking notice of the disappearances, though he doesn't say very much about them in front of the council. I'm told he's having Hemsgrid and Oldart go out to investigate in secret."

"Do they know anything of us or our plans?" Talis had heard a great deal about those two men. They were apparently the only people the king trusted without reservation.

"I don't believe so, no. If one of them knew, the king certainly would. They don't keep anything from him." Kels paused. "Are you certain they can't be used to our advantage, Talis? It would certainly make things–"

Talis' eyes burned as he made eye contact with Kels, Dormastis' frustration fueling his own. "Do you really think I would let them slip through the cracks if they were an option?"

Kels gulped and shook his head.

"No, of course I wouldn't," Talis continued. "Their hearts and minds are too pure, too focused on their work to think of anything else. We can control only those who seek what we offer and are too weak-minded to do anything about it themselves."

Kels coughed and cleared his throat, clearly not daring to say what he was thinking.

Fortunately, Dormastis knew. He always knew.

Talis offered a smirk in the candlelight. "No need to fret, Lord Kels. I speak only of those we find outside the castle walls. If you and the others suffered from weak minds, you certainly wouldn't be in your current positions."

Kels bowed in deference and tightened his cloak as he heard the door scraping to let other members of The Scythe into the chamber. He locked eyes with Talis once again. "For the Rebirth."

Talis smiled and savored the visible chill that went down Kels' spine as his golden mask smiled with him. "For the Rebirth."

Chapter Eleven

"Pardon my bluntness, but when men finally realize how insignificant they have become, women will rise and roar to rule like a great lioness of the plains of Dalheim. The male lion sleeps while the female hunts and raises the young. Imagine what she could do if the male were not there to hold her back."

-Entry from the Duchess Marania's personal diary

Marania stared defiantly at Talis' back. She'd been summoned quite abruptly. If one could define "summoned" as Lord Kels loudly knocking on her door and ushering her to the old dungeon first thing in the morning. She'd been preparing to attend a high council meeting. If she was tardy or absent without explanation, Steflan would be suspicious. As soon as Talis was finished, she intended to tell him exactly how she felt about the way she'd been treated.

Several minutes passed, and the silence was deafening. Marania was also unnerved by the absence of most of the other members of the Scythe. Their numbers had grown with each passing week, and she'd gotten used to the drafty room being full of people. She currently felt very exposed and vulnerable, though no less angry.

Finally, Talis spoke up from the shadows. His vexed tone did nothing to calm her. "My lady, I am...most disappointed in you. The plan should have been completed long before now. Dormastis has grown impatient. And so have I."

"What do you mean, my lord?" Marania asked. She was genuinely confused by his statement. "The plan was to push the king to the brink of mental collapse and let him be his own undoing. I just didn't anticipate his nerves to be so strong. And who could have predicted that the Havani would have the desire and cunning to oppose him? The Huntress is the—"

Talis whirled with an unexpected fury. "I speak not of the Havani or that pathetic imp they call the Huntress!" In an instant, his face was just inches from Marania's. She shrunk back as his hot breath touched her skin. "Dormastis is not pleased, lady," Talis hissed. "If Steflan is not finished soon, more drastic steps may have to be taken. We...*I*...could make things very unpleasant for you."

Marania's anger flared, and she felt her blood nearly boil in her veins. She jerked away from Talis. "How dare you speak to me in this way? I am your future queen! Furthermore, I'm the only one who knows who you all are. Do you honestly believe I will let you get away with threatening me once I have taken the throne?"

The duchess regretted her words the instant they came out of her mouth.

Talis grabbed her arm and pulled her close to him again. "Now, that's not entirely true, is it?" He whispered with a sneer. "Do *you* honestly believe you have any power here, woman? You have no idea who or what you are dealing with. Just do as we've told you, and you will rule this kingdom. I suggest you do it sooner rather than later. Do you understand?"

Marania couldn't breathe. Her heart felt as though it was about to pound right out of her chest. In the candlelight, the golden mask staring at her looked like it was on fire, making the painted expression even more sinister. She again jerked away from Talis and ran from the room. When she reached the top of the stairs, she slammed the door and stumbled to a nearby column, her breath shallow. Not for the first time since she began down this path, she felt that perhaps she was in over her head. Talis was right. He was the only member of the Scythe that she didn't know. Yet, that didn't change the fact that she would one day be queen. She would find out who this man was. Then, she would make him pay.

"What do you mean you were *outmatched*?"

The king asked his question incredulously, though the bruised and limping soldier before him had clearly taken a beating. The man's ill-fitting armor and lack of decorum told Steflan that he was one of the village recruits, but he knew nothing of his life or character. What the monarch did know was he was one of just a handful of survivors from a recent Havani raid. A raid from which all twenty men should have returned.

The great hall had been bustling with activity until the ragged soldier entered, as the members of the king's council had been meeting to discuss the Havani and the allocation of troops to cover all their needs. Between guarding the border pass, monitoring their current prisoners, patrolling all the villages, and the small contingents stationed in other kingdoms, Steflan knew his resources were stretched thin. Despite this, plenty of fully trained men were left to handle the Havani raids. At least, that's what he'd thought until hearing this report.

"Sire," The soldier continued. "You've heard of this Huntress, the one who's been ambushing our men?"

King Steflan rubbed his temples with frustration and groaned. "Yes, of course, I'm aware of some fool woman who's tried to overpower us. I wasn't under the impression she presented much of a threat. Most of our men have been returning from encounters with her, have they not?"

The soldier's eyes dropped to the floor, and he looked like he was trying to tie his fingers in a knot. He glanced nervously at Oldart, who strode up to the man and grabbed the back of his neck.

"What are you hiding, soldier?" Oldart growled.

"Well, Commander Ruskin said...he said as long as we replace the ones we lose, it's not important for you to know how many men she's killed..."

The king's eyes burned with silent ferocity. He turned to the young commander, who was leaning against a column by the doors. Steflan slowly stood and descended the steps that separated his throne from the rest of the room, approaching the man in question. "Do you mean to tell me you haven't been reporting all the men who have been killed by this rogue? You've just been replacing them with new recruits and hoping no one would notice?"

Ruskin hesitated and kept his malicious gaze on the poor soldier who'd given him away. "Yes, sire. I swear to you I meant no harm, I just thought-"

"You thought what?" Steflan's voice was rising rapidly, his anger swelling in his chest. "That I don't deserve to know the truth of the threat we're facing? How many soldiers are being wasted? How DARE you lie to me! Did you really think you would get away with this, boy?"

Oldart let the village soldier out of his grip and stormed toward Ruskin in a rage. "Sire, I can assure you I had no idea this was occurring. I would have put a stop to it immediately. Ruskin, how many men has she killed?"

Ruskin looked at the ground. "I'd say about half from every raid she's intercepted, captain. At least from those under my command."

Steflan's blood boiled. His face turning red, he balled his hands into fists to keep himself from personally strangling the commander in front of him. "Get him out of my sight," he ordered.

Oldart seethed with rage and embarrassment. He wasn't one to allow protocols to be ignored. "This man shall be severely punished, I can promise you." The captain gestured for two of his men to escort Ruskin to the dungeon.

With the commotion over, the hall was left silent, tense, and uncomfortable for all present. Steflan's eyes glared around the room, his menacing stare penetrating each courtier. "What else haven't I been told?" He bellowed almost maniacally around the chamber. "How many other secrets are being kept from your king?"

Not a single member of his court dared look him in the eye.

The agitated king moved to return to his throne. "Oldart," he motioned for him to follow. "I don't blame you for this man's behavior, but keep a closer eye on your officers. We cannot allow things like this to happen."

Oldart bowed and returned to his station by the door, through which Marania then swept, looking somewhat unnerved. She quickly composed herself and took her seat below the throne, followed closely by Lady Enid.

Steflan eyed his sister-in-law suspiciously as he sat back down. *It's not like her to be late for anything.* He would have to ask after her whereabouts once the meeting concluded. For now, he turned his attention back to the village soldier who still cowered before him.

"What's your name, soldier?"

"Euan Iker, Your Majesty. I come from the city of Vitalga, just beyond the castle walls."

"Very good, Euan. I thank you for your service to the crown. Now, can you tell me everything you remember about this Huntress? All I've been told is that she exists. I need to know exactly what we're up against. You personally faced her in combat, and you're the only one who's dared to be candid with me about it."

Euan nodded and began to recount the battle. "She wore a hood, and her mouth was covered, so we couldn't see her face, but her hands were visible. She is most definitely of the Havani race. Her skills are impressive, both with a bow and a sword."

"I can see that from your wounds," the King acknowledged. "What are her methods? Did she attack before you approached the tribe or wait until you initiated?"

"She didn't show up at all until the fight began. I've heard she never attacks before we do. They must have been following us for a while."

"They?"

"She has a companion she travels with, sire. A young man, by the looks of it."

"Is he also Havani?"

"No." Euan scratched his head thoughtfully. "His face was also covered, but from what I could see, he is of Enderen descent. He fights just about as well as she does."

"Hmm." Steflan became thoughtful. *Whoever he is, this young man is brazenly breaking the law, fraternizing with our enemy. We'll need to deal with him accordingly when we can.* He turned his attention back to Euan. "You don't remember anything else about what she looks like? I know there are wanted posters out and about, but I don't know if anyone has actually seen her."

Euan cleared his throat and shifted his weight from one leg to the other. "The only other thing I can tell you is she's very small. I'd say she doesn't stand even as tall as my shoulder."

The king leaned forward in his seat and narrowed his eyes, observing Euan's average height. "Are you telling me that this warrior, who's been killing my men and undermining my rule, is a child?"

"I don't think she's a child, Majesty." Euan gulped. "But I would guess she's rather young."

Steflan let out an audible growl. "Obviously, we need to bolster our forces to combat this *girl*, as loath as I am to admit it."

Oldart blinked furiously, a pained expression clouding his face. "What would you have us do, my king? We're stretched to our limits as it is. I'm afraid we would have to sacrifice our other defense needs in order to bolster the raid parties, and I don't–"

"What about the village recruits? We could increase the monetary incentive to volunteer. It's been at the current rate for a few years now. The promise of even more coin might entice those who are still reluctant to join us." Steflan was well aware he wasn't the most beloved monarch in the kingdom's history. Recruits weren't likely to sign up just to show their loyalty to the crown. However, if there was one thing he could count on from many of his subjects, it was greed.

Oldart swallowed hard and cleared his throat. "I know this won't please you to hear, Majesty, but the fact is your policies regarding the Havani are not terribly popular amongst the general population. Many are not inclined to volunteer no matter how much is offered, simply because they disagree with your, I mean, our methods." He looked as if he had more to add but chose to value his continued existence over proving a point.

From her perch below the throne, Marania shared a look with Enid, and her eyes darted around the assembly. After a few moments of internal panic, a small smile crept into the corners of the duchess' mouth. She stood and approached the king. "If I may interject, Your Majesty, I would say that if new recruits are reluctant to come willingly, we must remove the privilege of choice."

Steflan looked at her with a quizzical expression. "Are you suggesting conscription?

"That's exactly what I'm suggesting." Marania smiled. "If money alone doesn't compel, the law will. We can't pretend this will be an easy road, and many of our people will surely be unhappy. If it works, however, it could very well lead to the end of this terrible war with the Havani and the continued prosperity of Enderhail."

Steflan studied her face briefly before turning back to Oldart. "I want notices posted in every village that every able-bodied man from age sixteen to twenty-five must immediately report to the castle barracks for training. Anyone who resists is to be arrested and charged with treason."

Oldart stuttered before answering. "Your Majesty, are you quite sure that's wise? I'm sure Lady Marania means well, but I'm not certain she fully comprehends–"

The king rose abruptly and interrupted him. "I said," he commanded, "post the notices."

Oldart looked sternly at Marania before offering a bow to King Steflan and striding from the room.

Steflan gave Marania an unexpected nod of thanks, her tardiness forgotten, and gestured to the rest of the room. "You're all dismissed for now."

As the room began to empty of courtiers, Hemsgrid nervously approached the king. "Sire, do you think it wise to continue your assault on these tribes? Their numbers are dwindling, and few have dared to strike against you. Perhaps we should consider allowing those who remain to leave the kingdom and never return. At least then–"

The king sharply cut him off. "They took my son. I'm not convinced they weren't also responsible for the death of my queen. They undermine my leadership solely by existing. Death is too kind of a punishment for their crimes. I show them mercy in what I do. If you disagree, you are free to join them in their fate."

Hemsgrid bowed his head silently and took his leave. The old man's mind drifted as he made his way down the corridor. He'd known Steflan since birth and advised his father before him. He'd been the one who brought him to this kingdom to marry Alyssandra all those years ago. Yet the man before him now was unrecognizable. The advisor was convinced the king would destroy himself if this madness continued. He couldn't bear such a thought.

Back in the great hall, Steflan took one more quick glance around and noticed small clusters of people still chatting, no *whispering,* amongst themselves. They were probably gossiping about the arrogant and foolish acts of Commander Ruskin. Then again, he had noticed several people missing from the meeting, not for the first time. Could it be true? Were there other things he wasn't being told? The king wasn't one for paranoia, but the morning's events had definitely put him on edge. All this, combined with the recent reports of the string of mysterious disappearances from the surrounding villages, added to his mounting suppositions that something wasn't right. He made a mental note to ask Hemsgrid if he knew of anything suspicious. *Right after I apologize for speaking to him so harshly.*

Chapter Twelve

"It seems that many of the Havani tribes have been using an organized series of hideaways in order to elude my men. I have dispatched scouts to three of those known locations to gather information, especially as it pertains to the Huntress. Last night, I received a report that a particular tribe is harboring a young man who is not of their race. It's unclear if this is the same young man who has been colluding with the Huntress, but regardless, his association with the tribe is unlawful. Tomorrow, I am sending a company to their last known location with orders to find the tribe and attempt to bring the misguided Enderen back to the castle with them."

-Diary of King Steflan

Falling snow had never deterred a Havani tribe from their morning chores, and this day was no different. The large clearing now occupied by the Fortista tribe bustled with activity as families worked together to unload wagons, set up tents, and cook food. This new site was the second one in Chief Fortista's network that he'd been able to share with his daughter. She was thoroughly impressed with the level of leadership he'd maintained during the turmoil of her absence.

Xanya smiled at her father and took an empty crate from him, tossing it up into the wagon. Doing her part of the work felt so natural, as if she'd been doing it her whole life. The past several days had been like a dream for both Fortistas. They had talked and shared like those ten years apart had never happened. She and Dominic had even ridden out several times to continue their mission of saving tribes, often with a few of the tribe's scouts for support. The chief still wasn't entirely convinced she was doing the right thing, but he'd given up trying to discourage her from it.

Rafayel stared at his daughter's face and sighed contentedly, as he had done so many times since she'd returned home. Every morning, he feared he'd wake to find her gone, that his newfound happiness had been nothing more than a cruel nightmare. Yet every morning, she'd been there, emerging from the tent she shared with Emmaline and greeting him with the smile he'd missed more than even he'd realized.

The chief gently stroked Xanya's hair. "After everything that happened, I still can't believe Balthazar found you. Of all people! If I couldn't raise you myself, I feel blessed to know that he could. Thank the Sorcerers!"

"He was a good man." Xanya smiled sadly. "He made me and Dom into who we are. *I* still can't believe you never mentioned him! He was your and Mama's best friend."

Rafayel shook his head regretfully. "You should have known him sooner and under better circumstances. So much happened in my life. I wish...I wish I could have seen him again before he died. It just got harder and harder to muster up the energy to visit him, especially after your mother's death. I was afraid the memories of the three of us would be too painful." His eyes welled up, and he reached for his handkerchief in his pocket. "I should have had the wisdom to know those memories would have brought joy along with the pain, even amid the attacks. Then I would have found you sooner as well."

"Well, it would have been quite a shock to find you at our door," Dominic chimed in as he approached with an armful of wood and a grin on his face. "It's not often that legendary figures come back from the dead."

Xanya gave her friend a smirk and a small shove, but she knew he was being sincere. Before Balthazar, her father had been her hero; she'd always spoken of him as such. Rafayel had been nothing but a grand vision in Dominic's head. Now, here he was, talking to the man as though he'd known him all his life.

Rafayel laughed loudly and clapped the young man on the shoulder. "I don't often respond to flattery, but I'm in a good mood today, so I'll take that one." He tweaked his daughter's nose before leading Dominic into the center of the camp to build up the fires, their light-hearted conversation continuing as they went.

Xanya beamed with pride as she watched the two men she admired most enjoying one another's company so much. If only Balthazar could have been there to complete the joyous scene.

"Your father hasn't been this happy since before you disappeared."

Xanya jumped as Emmaline approached to wrap her cousin in a warm hug. "I know you don't remember your mother very well, but I do. You look so much like her."

The Huntress laughed as they pulled apart and started towards the fires. "You have no idea how many people have said that to me."

"I'm sure I do. Everyone who knew Aunt Ravenia can see it. I know that's one of the reasons Uncle is so happy to have you back. Not only are you alive and well, but he feels like maybe he didn't let her down after all."

"He did the best he could." Xanya shrugged. "Mama understands that. I don't believe for one second that he let her down."

Her smile faded, and she rolled her eyes as she noticed Dominic was flocked by several young women of the tribe. It had been a common occurrence since they'd settled in. She didn't know why she let it bother her so much. If those girls wanted to foolishly fall all over themselves, that was their business. However, she took a mild satisfaction in that he wasn't paying them any attention beyond a polite smile.

Emmaline gave her a knowing glance and cleared her throat. "Now tell me again, you just found him? You've never figured out who he is?"

"Balthazar found him wandering in the woods a few days before I stumbled upon him. They'd been separated, and he got stuck in one of my traps. And no, we never did find out where he came from. Balthazar looked for his family but never turned anything up. It doesn't bother him, though. He doesn't care where he came from, and neither do I. He's just Dominic. I'm very grateful to have him." Xanya abruptly stopped in her tracks and grabbed Emmaline's arm, her eyes flashing brightly. "Get the weapons."

Her cousin's expression darkened. "What?"

Xanya raised her voice to be heard through the camp. "Get your weapons! Now!"

She pulled her hood up and furiously unsheathed her sword as a band of soldiers burst through the trees, the largest company she'd seen so far. *Of course, the king left spies! We never should have stayed!* Around her, the tribe didn't flee but scrambled for anything they could use to defend themselves. Despite the situation, Xanya felt strong pride for her people. *They want to fight. They want to survive.*

As Xanya fended off a burly man who'd come at her with a spear, she heard a familiar cry of pain break through the chaos. She turned toward the sound just in time to see Dominic's shoulder get sliced open with a dagger. With a yell of frustration, she jumped just high enough to elbow her opponent in the throat. He sucked in a labored breath and dropped to the forest floor before Xanya ended his misery with her weapon. She then headed straight for Dom, who caught her eye over his attacker's shoulder.

"I'm fine! Help him!" He pointed behind her.

She followed Dom's gaze to the other side of the camp and gasped in horror as she caught sight of her father. He was on the ground, furiously waving his sturdy crutch about as he tried to deflect beatings from the soldiers surrounding him. His face twisted with pain as a mace came down repeatedly on his abdomen, his injured leg feebly attempting to kick the weapon out of the way.

Xanya's eyes blazed with unfettered rage. She stormed through the mayhem towards the downed chief, killing two more of the king's men as she went. The soldier standing at her father's head raised his club as she approached him from behind. She noticed his backplate dangling from one shoulder and took advantage of the damaged equipment, ripping it free and plunging her sword straight through his back. The soldier stiffened and dropped his weapon to the side before collapsing with a thud. His sudden demise distracted his comrades long enough for Rafayel to scramble to his knees and crawl away, dragging his bad leg behind him.

"You're all going to pay for that." Xanya's voice dripped with venom as she eyed the half-dozen pathetic men crowded around her. "Now, which one of you wants to go first?"

Xanya walked gingerly through the ruined Havani camp, stepping over rubble and surveying the damage through the smoke and blood-stained banks of snow. This attack was the bloodiest she'd seen, though the king's men only stayed long enough to kill about half the tribe. *Only.* With a heavy heart, she scanned the faces of the bodies she came upon, some dead, some still clinging to life. The pain and anguish on their faces brought hot, angry tears to her eyes. This was all her fault. She should have realized that staying potentially put all of them in jeopardy. But she'd only been thinking of herself and her own happiness at being reunited with her family. Now, they were all paying the price for her selfishness.

As she approached Emmaline and some of the elders, she spotted a figure on the ground that made her heart drop into her stomach.

Dominic.

Xanya ran the last few yards and fell to her knees, the tears that stung her eyes finally spilling down her cheeks. Blood dripped from the open wound on Dom's left shoulder and a cut on his lip, to say nothing of the developing bruises that covered his face and neck. He had never looked so fragile. She gently moved his head from the cold ground into her lap and heaved a sigh of relief as he winced in pain. He was alive. "Dom?" she whispered, gently brushing his damp brown hair out of his eyes, which slowly fluttered open.

His lips twisted into a pained smile. "Hey," he said weakly, clearly happy to see his friend. He noticed her tears, and concern washed over his face. "Shh, hey, I'm fine. You know I've looked worse."

Xanya gave a small snort of laughter. "You mean like when Balthazar took us to visit his cousins, and you fell in their pig pen?"

"Exactly." He grinned. "Ah." He groaned and shifted slightly, struggling to alleviate his discomfort. "You should probably go talk to your father. Emmaline said she'd be back to wrap these. At least if I die, it will be from nothing worse than blood loss."

Xanya frowned. "Don't even joke about that," she said flatly. "Don't you dare leave me."

Dominic cringed as he smiled again. "I wouldn't dream of it."

Xanya took off her cloak and balled it up, shoving it under his head to replace her knees. "I'll be back after I speak to my father." She stood and continued towards Emmaline's small crowd.

Rafayel had also approached Emmaline and was in the middle of a sentence when he noticed Xanya. He excused himself from his niece to pull his daughter aside. He glanced around the decimated camp before locking eyes with Xanya. His stare was not one of anger or disapproval but of despair. The pain from his beating was evident on his aging face. He leaned heavily on his crutch, though he displayed no outward injuries. Xanya was shocked he was even strong enough to stand.

"Papa, this is all my fault." She hung her head, struggling for the words. "We should have left days ago. This is why we don't stay with the tribes we help. Someone must have seen that we stayed on after the first attack and sounded the alarm. When Dominic is well enough to travel, we'll leave. I can't risk putting you all in danger again."

"What will you do? Continue to put *yourself* in danger for a lost cause?" Rafayel's face hardened into a glare.

Xanya felt her stomach drop. "Yes, I will. I know you disapprove of what I'm doing, but I made a promise and intend to keep it."

"Who did you make that promise to, child?" Rafayel's tone was becoming short. "To the Sorcerers? That you would meet them in the heavens before your time? I assure you that nothing but more pain and suffering will come out of this endeavor. One day, it might be your own."

"There are droves of Havani left in this kingdom. Dom and I have seen them. I know we're not fighters by nature, but if we just come together, we can make–"

"Then you would doom us all!" The chief yelled and startled those nearby. He took a deep breath to calm himself and grasped Xanya's shoulder, speaking so only she could hear him. "We have survived this long by existing only in the shadows. That's why I instituted the hideout system, which is now compromised, I might add. If we come together and fight, they will wipe us all out instantly. An entire way of life will be extinct. I can't allow that to happen. And I can't allow you to continue to put yourself at risk. Someday, and it may not be far off, I will no longer be here. As my heir, you will have to lead our people. It's what you were born to do."

Xanya was taken aback by this declaration, and she frowned. "But Emmaline has been the one by your side all these years…"

"I have spoken to Emmaline and the other elders. They agree the mantle must be passed to you, my daughter."

"Papa, I never intended to stay indefinitely. I must do what I can to raise my army and fight the king. That has always been my plan. I know I'm putting myself in danger, but if there's even a slight chance of ending this senseless violence, it will be worth it."

The distraught Havani chief tried to find the words to respond but gave up and simply pulled his child in for a hug.

She held him tightly and squeezed her eyes shut, savoring the embrace that had only existed in her dreams for so long. "I love you, Papa."

"Xanya, I–" her father stopped short as he pulled away.

Xanya looked up in alarm to see a small trickle of blood coming from the corner of his mouth. As she reached up to brush it away,

Rafayel's face paled as if completely draining of blood. He began to collapse, eyes wide and clouding over.

"Papa! Are you alright? What's wrong?" Xanya tried in vain to stop his fall, her much smaller body unable to bear his weight as they sank to the ground. Rafayel's breath came short and shallow as he went into shock, his body shaking as he reached for her hand.

"Help! Somebody help!" Xanya cried out desperately, willing her father to sit up and be well. "Just hold on. We'll get the healers to take care of you." Feeling utterly powerless, she tried to remain calm as others crowded around and offered their help. Tears started to pour down her cheeks once again, and she grasped his hand as tightly as she could.

Rafayel reached up with his free hand to stroke his daughter's cheek and attempted to give her a smile as his own eyes filled with tears. "You...you found us,' he murmured weakly. "You came home. If nothing else, I am grateful for the little time I had with you. Your mother..."

"Shh," Xanya said, her voice quavering as she tried to smile back. "Don't talk like that. You're going to be alright. You've always been the strongest of us. Besides that, I've only just come home. So you're not allowed to say goodbye yet."

The chief shook his head and grimaced as more blood came from his mouth. "I love you, my little warrior." He took a rasping breath. "You must be strong...for me....for them."

"I promise." Xanya let out a sharp breath. "But not yet. I still need you. You can't go now. Just hold on."

His grip loosened on his daughter's hand as Chief Rafayel Fortista took his last breath, his soul finally free of the pain he'd endured for so long.

"No, you can't go. No!" Xanya grabbed her father's shoulders and buried her face into his coat, her tortured screams muffled by the thick fabric. This wasn't happening. As long as she held onto him, it couldn't be over.

The rest of the tribe began to gather around curiously, panic passing through the ranks as people realized what was happening. Xanya fought back as hands grasped her shoulders and attempted to move her away. "No, I won't leave him! Let me go!"

Someone finally managed to gently pull Xanya to her feet so the healers could check the body. She stood motionless in the throng and couldn't breathe, unable to tear her gaze from her father's lifeless face. Her heavy heart thundered in her ears, and the whole scene swam before her eyes.

"Xanya!" Dominic was struggling through the crowd to get to her, blood still coming from his wounds.

She slowly turned at the familiar sound of his voice and stared right through him, indifferent to the people rushing around and jostling her from side to side. Before Dom could reach her, Xanya's eyelids fluttered closed. She fell unconscious, parting the crowd and hitting the forest floor beside what remained of her father.

Chapter Thirteen

"To those left behind, death may feel like an ending. It is merely a new beginning. It is a time for the soul to be free of mortal cares and pain, to comfort loved ones in spirit, and to lead them where they're meant to go. If they learn to listen carefully enough, they will hear you."

-Havani lore

Xanya sat on a small ridge overlooking the camp, knees pulled up to her chin. Her bloodshot eyes had run out of tears to cry. The cold seeped up from the frozen ground into her very bones, but she scarcely noticed the chill. Every inch of her body was already numb. Try as she might, she was unable to banish her father's corpse from her memory. At this moment, she thought his blank, blue eyes would haunt her for the rest of her days.

She twisted her fingers around the leather cord that secured a small vile hanging from her neck. Her eyes narrowed as she peered at the dark contents. The ashes were still warm. How could her father, so tall and strong, have been reduced to this pile of black dust? She shook her head in disbelief. It wasn't possible. It *shouldn't* be possible.

Losing her father felt different from losing Balthazar. Her thoughts drifted to that night so many months ago when she and Dom held their guardian's hands as he passed away peacefully in his sleep. His death had been just as sudden, but they'd known about his progressing illness for years. It was no surprise when his body no longer had the strength to fight, and he took to his bed. A few days more, and he was gone. They cried as they buried him next to their little cabin, with a small headstone that simply read, "Balthazar Gregriss, beloved guardian and friend." They grieved for him every day but were comforted by the years of happy memories they shared. With her father, she didn't have that solace. They had precious little time together. He died abruptly, painfully, and in turmoil. Worst of all, it was her fault.

She wasn't even able to give him a proper funeral. The bodies of Havani chiefs were traditionally taken to the top of the tallest waterfall in the kingdom to be burned. Mourners sang songs and prayed until the ashes were cool enough to be poured over the falls' edge. The water scattered them all across the kingdom, where they would help sustain the land that had sustained them in life. The small amounts of those ashes reserved for the family were placed in vials and blessed by the elders. It was a reminder that their bonds could never be severed, even in death.

That was the memorial Rafayel Fortista deserved, like the chiefs who had gone before him. Unfortunately, the tallest falls in Enderhail were close to the castle. The journey was a risk few Havani had been willing to take since the attacks began. Xanya supposed he wasn't the only deceased chief who'd had to settle for a simple pyre in the woods and a trip down the nearest river. She wasn't the first who'd been cheated of the opportunity to honor her dead, and she wouldn't be the last. It wasn't right.

Xanya wrapped her arms around her legs with a shiver, finally starting to feel the bitter temperature. She stared at her subdued tribe as they cleaned up the remaining mess from the battle and subsequent burials. They also grieved, but the work had to be done. Rafayel's death left a void in both their leadership and their extended family. Fortunately, they paid little attention to his daughter, sitting alone on the sidelines. She didn't want anyone giving her looks of pity or encouraging her to keep her chin up. She wanted her father back.

She didn't stir as Dominic came and painfully lowered himself to the cold ground next to her. Using his good arm, he draped Xanya's cloak over her back. It had only been a few hours, but he was already dying to get out of the bandages Emmaline had wrapped around his injured shoulder. His entire body was sore, but he was determined not to complain, especially in front of Xanya. His physical pain couldn't possibly compare to her sorrow.

They sat silently for a few minutes, watching the people go about their business and feeling grateful for one another's company. Part of Xanya wanted to talk to him, but she wasn't sure she had much to say. Nothing that was coherent, anyway. She hadn't even found the time to process the thoughts in her own head. How was she supposed to share them with someone else?

On the other hand, Dominic had quite a lot he wanted to say. Something had been bothering him for a while, something he didn't understand. Perhaps he'd been imagining things. Perhaps he hadn't. Either way, the man had to know.

He cleared his throat before he spoke. "You knew the attack was coming before it happened, didn't you?"

Xanya said nothing but nodded silently, keeping her gaze straight ahead.

The next question was the one that scared him most. "And that your father was going to die?" He braced himself for a range of emotional reactions.

Xanya hesitated before answering. "Well, I didn't know that. But I did know about the attack. Sometimes, I know a soldier's movements before they happen. Or I can feel if someone is sneaking up on me. I don't know how. It's like...I can sense things. Not all the time. It's happened my whole life. Honestly, I've never really thought much of it."

That was enough for Dominic to tentatively confirm his theory. "Xanya, I think you're a Seer."

She silently turned and looked at him, a quizzical expression on her tear-stained face.

"I know as well as you do how rare those abilities are," Dominic continued. "We've never come across a real one. Think about it, though. It would explain why you're so fast, why you know when certain things are about to happen, why I can never beat you at sparring." Dominic gave her an encouraging smile, hoping to draw her out of the emotional cage she'd trapped herself in.

In spite of everything, she returned the gesture, allowing the corners of her mouth to turn up just slightly before returning to her vacant expression. Dom had never seen her so withdrawn and timid, her usual ferocity buried in grief and uncertainty. Natural and necessary as these feelings were, he hoped she wouldn't let them overtake everything else she was.

"Maybe you're right." She exhaled slowly as she spoke, the words sounding resigned. "I don't suppose there's a way we can find out for sure. Even if it's true, I obviously can't control it. If I could..." She paused as she choked on the lump in her throat.

Dominic moved closer and put his arm around her. "I don't think you could have saved him, even if you'd known. The healers said–"

"I know what they said," she cut him off. "That doesn't help me."

The pair returned to their silence. Xanya played with the tiny vial of ashes in her hand and wished the world would just disappear. In her trance, she didn't even notice Emmaline approaching. She only looked up when Dominic nudged her to attention.

Emmaline wiped away tears as she came close. Xanya's cousin somehow looked to be under even more duress than herself. The Huntress supposed she understood. After all, Emmaline had spent far more time with her father than she had. When she lost her own parents in a raid, Rafayel was the only family she had left. Xanya imagined Emmaline felt the way she had when she ran away all those years ago. The sense of suddenly being alone in the world was a heavy burden.

"What shall we do now, Chief Fortista?" Emmaline's voice cracked.

Xanya sucked in a breath. "I'm sorry?"

"Your father is dead, Xanya. You are his heir. We follow your lead now." Emmaline gave a slight bow.

Xanya's mouth went slack, and she looked at Dominic in disbelief. "I...I can't do this, especially now. I'm not a leader." She turned back to Emmaline. "I'm not ready."

Emmaline smiled and offered a hand to pull Xanya to her feet. "You may not be, but it's your birthright and destiny. Uncle knew that. So do our people."

As she stood, Xanya noticed the rest of the tribe had stopped what they were doing to stare at the three of them. She tried to meet each and every gaze as she stared back. She saw their sorrow, but she also saw strength, pride, and hope. Hope they'd harbored for so long, never daring to express it out loud. Hope that could drive them to fight for a better future. Xanya's numbness began to melt away at the thought. Her father didn't want to fight. But she believed the people did. If he truly wanted her to be strong, she would have to go against his wishes. The time for mourning was over, at least for now. She had to finish what she started. With a reluctant smile, she finally turned back to Emmaline. "I'll do my best to follow in his footsteps."

Chief Xanya Fortista offered her people a nod and gestured for them to continue their work. Her eyes went to the snow-covered mountains in the distance, clouds spilling over their peaks and obscuring their majesty. Even without the fog, so much was hidden in those gargantuan walls. If they were going to fight, they would need help. She knew where they might be able to get it.

Xanya turned to Dominic, standing taller, her eyes sparkling faintly with hope once again. "I need to go on a little trip. I hope you'll come with me."

"Am I allowed to ask where we're going?"

"Not until we leave. Just trust me." She extended a hand to help him up.

Dom took it and got to his feet with a small grunt of pain. "I'm right behind you, Chief."

Appearing content with her decision, Xanya turned to make travel preparations. She only managed to make it a few yards before hanging her head and sinking her face in her hands. Dominic got off the ground and hurried forward as he saw her shoulders droop and begin to shake, her sobs bleeding through her fingers. She buried her face in his shoulder, and he held her tightly, resting his head on top of hers. His heart ached for his friend. She'd tried so hard to be strong that day, keeping her emotions inward as much as possible. Perhaps before they left, it would be best for her to shed the armor and acknowledge the truth: that she was just a child who'd lost her father. Again.

Chapter Fourteen

"*They came out of nowhere. Nothing more than drunken thugs who seemed bent on the destruction of this tribe. Nyra is recovering, thank the Sorcerers, but she lost the child. Our child. Nothing can ever make that right. The rest of the tribe may not agree, but I don't believe this kingdom is safe for us. Not anymore. I intend to find us a new home, somewhere this atrocity will never happen again. If, somehow, it does, I will ensure we're ready.*"

-Kerrigan's tribal logs

The wind howled, and snowflakes stung their faces as the two young warriors hiked further into the blizzard that whipped around them. Xanya pulled her scarf more tightly around her mouth and nose, then turned to make sure Dominic was still behind her. They left their horses at the base of the mountains three days earlier and spent their nights in the same caves she and her father had when making this journey many years ago. She was surprised she remembered the way, even in this stormy mess.

On the other hand, Dominic had no idea where they were going. All Xanya told him was they needed to go north. But how much farther north could they go before they left Enderhail altogether? Dominic pulled his scarf down, attempting to be heard over the gale. "Just how far north did you mean?" He shouted. "I wouldn't be surprised if we fell off that supposed edge of the world at any moment!"

Xanya turned and waited for him to catch up with her. "Not too much farther," she assured him. The wind died down temporarily, allowing them to speak more freely. "Yes, it's out of the way, but it's how Kerrigan and his tribe have survived for so long. King Steflan and his armies probably don't even know they exist. Sorcerers, I doubt some of my own people remember them. They've been up here for around forty years."

"Do you really think this is a good idea?" Dominic asked incredulously. "If they wanted to intervene, they could have done it long before now. Like you said, they're pretty far away from civilization. This isn't really their fight. Wouldn't it be more beneficial for them to continue hiding away?"

Xanya nodded in agreement. "I suppose you're right. But one thing I remember is that nothing is more important to Kerrigan than family and the safety of our people. Trust me, he'll help us. C'mon, we have to keep going." She took his arm, and they started forward again as the wind picked back up.

Dominic let her lead the way and placed the scarf back over his mouth and nose, hiding the smile that resulted from being so close to her.

Xanya was navigating by a solid rock wall on their right, its crags twisting into the cloudy oblivion. Her eyes followed the curvature of the wall, and she gave a small squeak of excitement as she finally saw where it turned sharply inward, directing them into the very heart of the mountain. A shivering Dominic stared rigidly at the ground, and Xanya had to pull on his arm to adjust his course.

As they rounded the corner, they were met with a stony downward slope, which leveled out at the enormous mouth of a cave. The cliffs that now surrounded them offered a much-needed reprieve from the storm. Xanya furiously tried to rub the chill out of her arms and pulled the scarf away from her face. This was the beginning of the end of their long, unexpected journey.

They half slid, half walked down the ice and snow-covered ground, precariously holding one another for balance until they reached the mouth of the cave. It was impossibly large, like the gaping maw of some hidden creature just waiting to swallow them up. Xanya faintly remembered approaching this cave with her father as a small child, fearing that was precisely what was about to happen. He'd reminded her of their people's belief that the mountains grew out of Enderhail's desire to protect its land and people from harm. *The mountains*, his voice echoed in her mind, *are a fortress full of secret passages and hidden corridors. The more you explore them, the more wonders you might find.*

The memory brought a smile to her face and a tear to her eye. She clutched her chest as the ache of his absence began to creep back in. *I know you didn't want me to do this, Papa, but I have to try.*

"You know I'm not one to complain," Dominic remarked, "but we've been hiking through a blizzard for three days. Wouldn't it be nice to get out of the cold?"

With her thoughts interrupted, Xanya realized she'd just been staring blankly at the cave entrance. The physical and emotional fatigue had finally started to outweigh her bout of adrenaline. She shook her head vigorously and tapped at her cheeks with gloved hands. *Wake up, Xanya.* "Sorry, Dom. I know we have to keep going. We can't *flake* out now." She grinned sheepishly at her play on words.

Dom gave her a pained smile and blinked slowly in response.

"Don't pretend I'm not funny," she said matter of factly. That comment drew a genuine smile out of him, the kind that made him inadvertently wrinkle his nose and caused her heart to skip a beat. Not that she ever planned on mentioning that fact to him.

Clearing her throat nervously, Xanya finally turned and entered the cave with Dom trailing behind. She reached into her pack to retrieve the supplies for lighting a torch. As the flame sputtered to life, the light bounced around the walls and the stalactites hanging from the high ceiling. Water dripping down the walls added a kind of dampness to the air and gave the whole place a slimy sheen. It was preferable to the storm outside, but not by much.

"Can you take this, please?" Xanya handed the torch to Dominic and pulled some sheets of parchment from her pack, worn and wrinkled pages that had been torn from their binding and were covered in a slanted scrawl. "I took these from one of my father's logbooks," she explained. "I knew he would have the directions somewhere." She took the torch back from him and started forward, going deeper into the cave and studying the parchment as she went.

"Directions for what?" Dominic asked skeptically as he hurried to keep up. He'd been good at hiding it, but Xanya could tell her secrecy was starting to annoy him.

"Directions through the tunnels," she answered. "Stay close to me, and whatever you do, don't go the wrong way."

What should have been the back of the cave branched off into two tunnels, one going right, one left. Xanya double-checked her map and led them down the path to the right, holding the torch as high and as far out in front of her as she could. After a few minutes, they came to another fork. This time, she took the left. The place was a maze. Fortunately, her father had had the foresight to note the correct path.

"I'm sorry I haven't told you my plans. I know it's been bothering you." She was glad of the darkness. Despite a desire to soldier forward, she was starting to doubt her decision to come and didn't want him to notice her growing apprehension.

"That's only because it's not like you to keep things from me. I was just getting worried." Dominic's words were sincere. It took much more than that to make him truly angry.

"I know, and I appreciate that. But the truth is this is much more of a risk than any interaction we've had with a tribe so far. I've only met this chief once. He was kind, but I don't know if he will agree to give us his army."

"Army?" Dominic sounded confused. "The Havani are peaceful. Why does this tribe have an army, especially when they are so far out of the way?"

"Kerrigan's tribe has been up here since they were attacked around forty years ago."

"Forty years?" Dom frowned. "But the old king was still in power then. I thought he didn't have any issues with your people."

"It wasn't the king. They were just a bunch of drunken bullies who hated us and finally decided to do something about it, I guess. King Thane even tried to find who did it and arrest them. He never did, though."

"So one attack was enough to get Kerrigan to abandon his home and traditions? That doesn't sound like the Havani way."

Xanya looked over her shoulder. "His wife, Nyra, was injured. She lost her baby." She started forward again.

"So he decided finding a new home and creating an army was the best way to keep something like that from happening ever again." Dom shook his head in dismay. "Why didn't more tribes go with them? Things might be different today if they had."

"At the time, there was no reason for us to go. Even now, simply staying in the valley is how we hold on to our heritage. I guess it's fighting back in its own way. But when Karrigan wanted to leave, many of the chiefs saw him as a coward. Not even all of his own tribe went with him, though branches of several other tribes did. My grandfather was one of the few chiefs who didn't condemn him for his decision. He brought my father here a few times when he was growing up, and my father brought me. I only came once. Kerrigan is a distant cousin, and it was their way of trying to keep the family together. I'm hoping he'll remember the kindness we showed him, and it will convince him to help."

They continued in silence for several minutes. Xanya checked her notes every time they came to another fork. The tunnels were wide enough that Dominic eventually moved beside her to take the torch with his good arm, holding it so she could still see her father's scrawled handwriting as they went.

Beginning to feel bored, Dominic started humming and dancing the torch around to his tune, the shadows from the flame bouncing happily in the gloom of the passage.

Xanya squinted at the directions and turned to him, grinning in spite of herself. "Stop!" She tried to hide her chuckle as he thrust the torch toward her like a sword. "I can't read these when you do that. We can't afford to get lost in here. We'd probably never find our way out."

"Sorry." He laughed, his voice echoing around them. "I could tell you were getting into one of your moods. I needed to pull you out before you were too far gone." Changing the subject, Dominic raised the torch to study the towering ceiling of the cave. "Do you still believe Balthazar's story that there's nothing beyond these northern mountains? Or to the west? All the other kingdoms are partially bordered by the ocean. Why shouldn't that be true here, even if we can't get over this part of the range?"

"The world begins and ends with Enderhail," Xanya smirked, quoting a verse from one of the history books Balthazar used to teach them.

"C'mon, Xanya, I'm serious. There's no earthly reason for these mountains to mark the end of the world."

"Who said it was an earthly reason?" Xanya waggled her eyebrows mysteriously in the torchlight. "That ancient explorer was convinced he'd get to the other side and find a new kingdom for him and his family to rule. No one ever heard from him again."

Dominic shrugged dismissively. "He was a lone traveler crossing a massive mountain range! Of course, his chances of survival were slim. Anyone who thought he was coming back was a fool."

Xanya pointed a finger at him. "What about what happened to his wife and children?"

"Oh yes, I'm certain they disappeared into thin air in the middle of a crowded tavern. Poof." Dom waved his fingers sarcastically, making Xanya giggle. "I'm not even sure I believe that happened. It was hundreds of years ago."

"You think I have the power to See the future, but you don't believe that story? My friend, you have a very specific threshold for believing in magic." Xanya poked him playfully in the side.

"Yeah, yeah." He stuck his tongue out at her.

The ground beneath their feet started to incline upwards, and Xanya gulped. "We're almost there."

The blackness of the tunnels began to melt away, and the musty air became fresh. They finally rounded a corner to find the opposite end of the maze they'd been traversing. Dominic shoved the torch into a pile of snow as they stepped out of the cave, the flames extinguishing with a hiss. Squinting in the white light, they stood still for a minute to get their bearings.

The mouth of the cave was at the bottom of a small hill. There was no wind here. They may as well have imagined the raging storm on the other side of the mountain. They wove their way through the pine trees that dotted the hillside and paused again at the top. Dominic let out an audible gasp as he saw what lay below.

Stretched out before them was a large valley, perfectly carved into the space between the tall peaks that surrounded them on all sides. Clustered amongst the sparse trees and vegetation were hundreds of tents and a few sturdy houses, smoke curling from each chimney. Fires dotted the encampment, and the air rang with the sounds of village life like nothing they'd ever experienced with other Havani. The ebony-haired, porcelain-skinned villagers went about their business, oblivious to the observing strangers. Amongst the recognizable traits, however, was one notable difference: every man, and most of the women, wore glinting silver armor. It was remarkably similar to what the king's men wore and, therefore, quite unsettling. Xanya marveled at how something could simultaneously be so familiar and so foreign.

"This is why we had to come here." She turned to Dominic in earnest, smiling at his slackened jaw. "You and I have given people the desire to fight back. Kerrigan and his men can help us give them the *tools* to fight back. The king will never see it coming." Xanya started striding down the hill towards the village.

"Wait!" Dominic stumbled as he hurried to catch up with her. "We're just going in there unannounced? Shouldn't we come up with a plan first?"

"We have a plan," she said matter-of-factly. "Talk to Kerrigan and get him to help us."

"What if he says no?"

Xanya stopped dead in her tracks and turned to him, face hardened and lips pursed. "He won't."

Dominic tried not to protest as she turned her back to him and continued her descent. He hoped, for both their sakes, that she was right.

As the ground beneath their feet leveled out, they were spotted by a tall woman patrolling the outskirts of the village. She put her hand on the hilt of her sheathed sword. "Who are you, and what do you want?"

"I am the warrior known as the Huntress," Xanya said in an impressive and confident tone. "I wish to speak with your chief. He will know me."

The young woman stared at them shrewdly. "Who's this handsome fellow?" She gestured to Dominic, who blushed.

"He is my bodyguard and friend," Xanya replied with their agreed-upon answer. "I trust him with my life."

The guard didn't soften her gaze but let go of her weapon. "Come with me. Don't follow too closely." She turned without another word and led them into the midst of the tribe.

Xanya and Dominic followed their rigid hostess through the crowds of Havani, very aware of the dozens of pairs of eyes watching them. Xanya's nerves rose steadily, but she knew everything would be alright once she saw Kerrigan.

After several minutes, the armored woman turned and gestured for them to stop in front of a large tent that was fenced off from the rest of the tribe. "Wait here." She left them outside the fence while she walked up the crudely made rock path and into the structure.

Xanya started to tremble, her stomach tying itself in knots. Why did she feel so tense? She'd felt so confident this would be easy. Kerrigan was one of the kindest men and chiefs she'd ever met. She remembered his warm smile and welcoming spirit from her childhood. His tribe, too, had been so open, the people lively and happy despite their constant readiness to fight. So what was different? Something just felt...wrong. She cast a sidelong glance to Dominic, who saw the concern on her face and furrowed his brow, attempting to read her expression. She gestured behind them with her eyes, asking a silent question.

Dominic nodded and subtly turned to find themselves surrounded by a wall of armed men and women, weapons at the ready. His eyes widened as he slowly turned back to Xanya, shaking his head slightly with alarm. It was too late to avoid whatever was coming.

Finally, the tent flaps parted, and a group of men approached them. Xanya did not see Kerrigan in the company, although as they got closer, she recognized their leader and gagged internally. He was taller, leaner, and more muscular, but other than that, Kerrigan's son Jaheel was exactly as she remembered him. He wore a long black coat adorned with silver buckles, a loose-fitting white shirt underneath, black trousers, and a garish red sash tied around his waist. A sword hung loosely at his side, looking more like an accessory than a tool, and his sleek black boots shone as if they'd never seen a single day of work. Underneath the square jawline and short beard, Xanya could still make out the baby-faced bully he'd been when they were young. She remembered how much of her visit she'd spent avoiding the spoiled, thoroughly unpleasant older boy.

Physically attractive as Jaheel had become, it was overshadowed by the cloud of arrogance that hung over him. The smile became a sneer, the smoldering gaze became unsettling, and the swagger of confidence turned to one of self-importance. Xanya had seen similar behavior from a number of the king's men. This was not the kind of person she wished to engage with. Unfortunately, he appeared to be the one in charge. Perhaps this wouldn't be as easy as she had hoped. Unless he'd had a dramatic change of heart, Jaheel was nothing like his father. She prepared to attempt a genuine smile.

All of Xanya's resolve to be pleasant was washed away when the man opened his mouth.

"Well, well, well." Jaheel's honeyed voice spilled out of his sneering lips like sap dripping from a broken tree branch. "If it isn't my dear little cousin Xanya, back from the supposed grave. Or should I call you Huntress? It's been far too long." He opened his arms wide, obviously expecting her to embrace him.

Instead, Xanya grimaced and again scanned the crowd of Jaheel's cronies. Her eyes narrowed. "Where's Kerrigan?" she growled.

Lowering his arms, Jaheel sauntered closer and clicked his tongue disapprovingly. "Such hostility, even after all this time. I had hoped we could put all that unpleasantness behind us and be friends."

Xanya could no longer keep her disgust at bay. "What in the name of the Sorcerers would give you that idea?"

"People are not stagnant beings, Xanya. They grow and change, just like all living things. Perhaps if we spent a little more time together, you'd learn to like the person I've become." Jaheel gave her a subtle wink that she assumed was meant to be charming.

"I doubt anyone can change *that* much, Jaheel," her snarky reply earned a slight snicker from his gang. "Now where. Is. Kerrigan?"

Jaheel whipped around to glare at the crowd behind him, silencing their laughter, then turned back to Xanya. "My father is unavailable at this time. I am performing his duties as chief until further notice."

"And your mother?" Despite how she doted on him, Nyra would not likely be pleased with how her son was treating their guests.

"My dear, you know what losing my would-be older sister did to the poor woman. She's never away from my father's side. For now, this tribe is solely under my authority."

"Having authority is not the same thing as deserving it," Xanya retorted.

Jaheel pursed his thin lips and began to pace back and forth, stroking his whiskers. He directed the conversation away from the current line of questioning. "This is a long way for you to come, especially in such dangerous times. Is there something we can do for you, or are we going to continue wasting time with this hostile discussion?"

Xanya's resolve fluttered, and she turned to Dom with a look of trepidation. He squeezed her shoulder protectively and gave her a nod of reassurance.

Jaheel finally acknowledged Dominic for the first time. "Who's your friend?"

"Someone I trust," Xanya grunted. "I do have something to say if you'll permit me."

Jaheel smiled knowingly and settled on a nearby wooden stool, gesturing for her to continue.

Xanya stood a little taller and took a few steps forward, raising her voice to be heard by more of the assembly. "Our people have been under attack from King Steflan for over ten years. It's high time we fought back. Many of the valley tribes have finally expressed the will to do so. If we are to take our freedom back from this tyrant, we will need your help to form an army and teach them to fight. This may be our last hope of survival." She softened her gaze and tone, looking her distant cousin straight in the eye. "Please, Jaheel, will you do this for us?"

Without much hesitation, Jaheel rose and studied his visitors, arms folded over his chest. "You come from a troubled land, darling. Trouble follows those who make it. You, in particular, have become rather famous for that. If indeed you are this fabled Huntress, as you claim." Jaheel snapped his fingers at one of his thugs, who handed him a folded sheet of parchment. He glanced at it briefly and turned it towards his audience. "This looks nothing like you."

Xanya flinched at the all too familiar WANTED letters framing the page. "I'd say that's a stroke of good luck, wouldn't you?"

"Perhaps." The chief's son shrugged. "But I have no time to argue this matter any further. My answer is no."

Xanya was taken aback. "No?" She stuttered.

"No. We may have ample numbers and weapons, but the risk is too great. I want to protect my people just as you want to protect yours. Isn't that right?"

"I want to protect *all* of our people." Xanya's blood began to boil in her veins. "Are we not still one race? One culture? One family?"

The pompous young man before her suddenly seemed to realize something. "Speaking of family, why is it that you came and not your father? Is his poor leg still ailing him?"

Xanya drew in a sharp breath, tears stinging her eyes. "Since he recently died, no, I don't believe it is ailing him. Not anymore. I now command what remains of the Fortista tribes."

Jaheel's steely blue eyes looked Xanya up and down. He came to stand very close and circled her slowly. She tensed, and her eyes followed him rigidly, the scowl returning to her face.

"So you," his silver tongue attempted to crack her hard exterior, "a young woman, are planning to rule without a husband. That could prove to be difficult in this era of distress. You know, you have grown to be quite beautiful, cousin. Perhaps we could come to some sort of...arrangement that would be mutually beneficial." He reached up to stroke her cheek with his thumb, and she jerked away, her eyes turning to daggers.

Dominic lunged forward, hand on his sword. "Don't you dare speak to her that way," he said through clenched teeth.

Jaheel took a small step back and smiled again as Xanya held her friend behind her. "I'm only making an offer. You could have my army and all this," he gestured to himself grandly, "with one small word." He gave her what she thought was meant to be a smoldering look and waited patiently.

She let her jaw drop in disbelief and stared blankly at the man before her. Any physical appeal he had was diminished by his self-importance and chauvinism. *He's intelligent, I'll give him that. But how dumb does he think I am that he expects this little "offer" will work on me?*

Xanya softened her face into a sweet smile and sighed heavily. "Oh, my dear cousin," she said.

Dominic raised his eyebrows, and Jaheel nodded with satisfaction.

"You're just not worth the trouble." Xanya's smile turned smug, and the pig-headed young chief went slack-jawed. Xanya strode forward and got as close to his face as she could with her small stature. "My pride and self-respect are worth more to me than an army," she spat menacingly. "If this is the best your tribe has to offer, we'll find other means to accomplish our goal."

Jaheel's mouth hung open with shock. It was very likely no one had ever spoken to him that way.

Xanya gave him a final glare and condescendingly raised one eyebrow. "Your father would be *very* disappointed in you."

As Jaheel sputtered in disbelief, Xanya turned sharply on her heel and grabbed Dominic's hand, roughly pulling him through the stunned crowd. Even with all the horrors she had witnessed, she couldn't remember experiencing this kind of anger and disgust in her life. Her hands were clenched so tightly that her knuckles turned white, and Dominic could feel her shaking as he tried to pull away from her iron grip.

As they moved quickly back through the trees toward the tunnels, Dominic shook his head and tried to calm his friend, finally pulling his hand free. "Should we really give up so quickly? We came all this way! Shouldn't we give him more time to consider? Maybe if I–"

"No," Xanya said gruffly. "I refuse to give him the satisfaction of thinking we need him."

Dominic stopped walking. "...But we do need him."

Xanya whirled angrily, stomping on the damp ground as she approached him. All the rage and grief she'd been shoving into the pit of her stomach for so long came spilling out all at once. "Don't you think I know that?" She yelled. "I wouldn't have even tried coming here if we didn't need these people! At the very least, their weapons and expertise could give us better odds against the king. Unfortunately, the one person who would have been willing to help us isn't here. He may not even be alive." She paused. "We can't work with that..." She shook her head, unsure of how to finish the sentence. There wasn't a word she could come up with to adequately describe Jaheel's deplorable character.

"Xanya, come on. Stop." Dominic placed his hands on her shoulders, willing her to calm down. She'd never spoken to him so combatively. "I guess we'll have to figure out some other way. If we gather the people and work together, everything will be–"

"No," Xanya cut him off softly, sounding almost desperate. "No, nothing is going to be alright or fine. Nothing is going to work out. This was our last hope, Dom. Without this army...I don't think we have a chance." Tears ran down her cheeks as she jerked away from him and ran towards the hill.

Dominic stared after her, wishing he could do something, anything, to make this all go away. For the first time, he felt like there wasn't a single thing he could do for her. It had all just become too much. They were in for a very long journey home.

Chapter Fifteen

"I've determined, out of necessity, that solitude can offer peace and quiet to a troubled soul if used wisely. But if you're not careful, it can force you to confront who you truly are. If you don't know who that is, the solitude can become terrifying."

-Entry from the diary of Duchess Marania

"Alyss!" Marania cried out as she awakened and sat up, sweat dripping down her brow. Her sister's face faded from sight as her eyes darted around the dark room. *It was just another dream.*

She took the handkerchief from her night table and wiped her damp forehead, her hands shaking as she did so. Recently, it felt like she hadn't been able to think of anything but Alyssandra. Her face was in every mirror, her voice whispered in her ears. Some days, she even thought she saw her riding through the courtyard. It didn't help that there were still traces of her all over the castle, from the portraits hanging in various rooms to the possessions she'd left behind. The late queen was everywhere.

The duchess guzzled water from her bedside jug and tried to stop herself from hyperventilating. This dream had been just like all the others. It began with the two sisters as young girls, playing happily in their nursery and making up stories together. Just as they were about to clean up their playthings, a massive figure in a black cloak burst through the door and snatched Alyss away. Through her sister's screams, Marania struggled with the stranger and, with great difficulty, finally yanked down the hood. To her horror, underneath was her own face, twisted and menacing, eyes red as blood. The evil duchess kicked her off like a fly and dragged Alyssandra down the blackened hallway, leaving little Marania lying face down on the floor sobbing. Alyss' pleading cry would echo around her: *"How could you do this to me? Your own sister?"*

Marania would then wake up, shocked, terrified, and utterly heartbroken by the scene. The dream didn't come every night, but it came often enough. The nights she didn't dream of her sister were occupied by similarly dark thoughts of her nephew. Sometimes, she couldn't believe what she had done. Other times, she forgot about it completely, like her actions were a nightmare she could carelessly shove aside. She barely remembered what had been going through her head on those two nights. Had anything really happened at all?

"Of course it happened," she croaked to herself. She finally stumbled out of bed and was hit with a wave of overwhelming dizziness. Marania grabbed various objects for support as she made her way to the window. With some difficulty, she pushed it open to breathe in the cool morning air. She looked out at the sun beginning to rise over the mountains, the forest still bathed in the fading shadow of night. The air was cold. Spring was on the way, but winter still clung to the land. Marania noticed that despite the chill, she felt hot, and her forehead was moist with sweat.

It was in these still, lonely moments that Marania most often felt Alyss's presence dancing around her, like the scent of a perfume that lingered in the air after its wearer left the room. Strangely, that presence was never menacing or vengeful. It was instead mournful and full of questions. How could she have committed such a reprehensible act?

Because you knew it was the only way to get what you deserve.

That was what the voice in her head told her when she had these doubts. Doubts that made her question every decision she'd ever made. Despite the anger, confusion, and betrayal she'd felt when their father chose the younger Alyssandra to rule rather than her, she'd never imagined herself ending up in such a position. Had this really been her only option? The Scythe had led her to believe so.

After a few minutes of staring out the window, Marania's body started to tremble, and she found it hard to breathe. She carefully guided herself back to bed, ringing the bell for Prudence, her lady's maid, to come tend to her. Her thoughts returned to her childhood. Alyss had always been the kinder, more gentler soul than she. Her heart was as large as Enderhail itself, and she was always looking for ways to make others happy. Despite her husband's aloof demeanor, the late queen had been a light in the dreary castle. She'd smiled at everyone, which made her nose wrinkle in a way that could disarm even the most guarded heart. The kingdom had loved her. How could Marania have deprived the world of such a joyful spirit?

Because you knew it was the only way to get what you deserve.

Prudence knocked softly and entered, still in her nightgown and looking slightly eager. Marania rarely rang for her anymore. The poor girl had spent a good deal of time the last few years in the kitchens rather than doing her trained duties. Her face fell when she saw the duchess lying in bed so weakly, her eyes beginning to glaze.

"Oh, good heavens!" Prudence rushed to the bed and laid a hand on Marania's forehead. "My lady, you're burning up. Have you felt like this all night?"

Marania tried to speak but could only manage a belabored moan.

"Well, I suppose that doesn't matter," Prudence said as she gathered some items from around the room. "We need to take care of this fever at once." She hastily opened the remaining two windows in the room and took the damp blankets off the bed.

Marania's shivering intensified, and she opened her mouth to protest.

"I know it's cold," Prudence said. "But we need to get your temperature down. I'll be right back with some rags and hot broth. We'll get you back on your feet in no time."

Before the maid could leave the room, Marania finally choked out a few raspy words. "Please inform the king I will not be present at the meetings today. Send my apologies."

Prudence gave a curtsy. "I will tell Hemsgrid immediately." The young woman swept out, and Marania could hear her running down the hall to the back stairs.

Marania took slow, deliberate breaths, attempting to focus on the present rather than the distant past. At least she wasn't supposed to meet with the Scythe today. Talis always seemed so irritated when she could not attend their gatherings when assigned, yet was equally put out by her presence. They spoke of the progress with the king and the Havani, which she read right from her own transcriptions of the council meetings. She didn't know what the nomads still had to do with putting her on the throne, but Talis had repeatedly assured her the tactics were necessary.

What did the group do on the days she wasn't invited? Except for council meetings, which they were often late to or leaving early from, she didn't see those particular lords and ladies during the day anymore. They had to be up to something else. Once she was queen, she would ensure all the secrecy would come to an end.

When her head started to get fuzzy, Marania closed her eyes until she heard Prudence re-enter the room to cover her with fresh blankets and place a cool, wet cloth on her forehead. The lady's maid gave her mistress a few sips of broth before the duchess fell asleep, her mind swimming with thoughts of her terrible deeds and the hope that soon they would all be worth it.

Predictably, the trek back to Xanya's tribe was miserable for both her and Dominic. She stormed ahead, clearly not wanting to engage with him in any way. The two nights they spent in caves were silent, although Xanya did help him refresh his bandages once. It was reminiscent of their first day together all those years ago. Only this time, there was a new kind of tension between them. After everything they had been through, they just weren't used to feeling so awkward with one another.

Once they got out of the mountains, returning to the tribe was still a bit of a chore. After the events of that terrible morning, Xanya ordered Emmaline to move the encampment to a location that wasn't part of Rafayel's network of hiding places. He'd been right that it was now compromised, thanks in part to her carelessness. In their haste to leave, a specific meeting spot had not been arranged to return to the tribe. Xanya and Dom spent almost a day tracking from their last camp before they came upon Sertus' scouting route and followed him to their new site.

After a fitful night's sleep in her father's wagon, Xanya rose earlier than most and took a makeshift target into the woods with her quivers and bow. She knew she had to stay close to the tribe but wanted to be alone. If a few hundred feet away was all she could get for now, she'd take it.

She shot arrow after arrow into the center of that target, sometimes walking to retrieve it, sometimes letting the new one slice right through the shaft of her last shot. The pattern of *thunks* that rang out when the arrows hit their mark was oddly soothing to her frayed nerves.

As she practiced, she tried to remember the last time she and Dominic had gone so long without speaking, if there ever was such a time. Even their childhood spats had been short-lived. As they got older and Balthazar became sick, they realized that one day, they might only have each other to rely on. That thought alone was always enough to help them work out any disagreements that came along.

This time felt different. This time, it wasn't anger so much as a terrible impasse. There was nothing either one of them could do to move forward. Xanya knew none of it was his fault. But her desire to stay angry about the whole situation outweighed her desire to talk to him, apologize, and figure out what to do next. The world had been unfair and cruel to so many for so long. Why should she be any different? Her optimism hadn't helped much anyway. *I should talk to him. No, I should wait for him to talk to me.*

Thunk. Another arrow hit the target.

"Where was Kerrigan?" She asked herself out loud

Thunk.

"Why does Jaheel have to be such a pigheaded oaf?"

Thunk.

"Why did my father have to die?" She heard rustling behind her and whirled instinctively, bow poised to shoot. To her surprise, Dominic came through the bushes, his hands raised in a conciliatory manner.

"Emmaline said you came this way." Dom relaxed and ran his fingers through his hair as he came closer.

Xanya realized this was the first time she'd really looked at him since they left Kerrigan's tribe. The bruises on his face had faded, leaving yellow splotches behind and making him look rather ill. He had removed his leather armor, which Xanya never did herself, and his bandages poked through the top of his loose-fitting gray shirt.

"You look like you're healing. I'm glad." Xanya avoided making eye contact.

Dom jumped right to the point. "I'm sorry you got your hopes up for nothing. It was a long shot. You said so yourself. Of course, you *rarely* miss any shot you take." He grinned mischievously and grabbed an arrow from her quiver, twirling the shaft between his fingers.

Xanya snorted and rolled her eyes. In light of their recent string of bad luck, his willingness to return to the status quo irritated her. "Are you seriously making jokes at a time like this? When we have no idea where to go from here?"

Dominic put the arrow back and defensively held his hands up again. "Whoa, hold on. I was just trying to clear the air and cheer you up."

"There is no cheering me up," Xanya snapped. "Not when we're out of options. Even if all the remaining tribes in the valley join us, which they won't, it won't be nearly enough to march against the king. We needed that army! Now we're sunk." She shook her head in dismay. "I wouldn't expect you to understand. These aren't your people, and this isn't your fight. You have nothing to lose if it goes badly."

"Oh no, that's not fair," Dominic scoffed, raising his voice, "And you know it. These may not be my people, but I *chose* this because I know it's right. I choose it every single day. I am the *only* one who has been with you every step of the way and seen everything you have seen.

Your people have the right to be safe and free. That's why I fight. But make no mistake, the only other thing in this that truly matters to me is *you*." He pointed at her sharply, his index finger mere inches from her shocked face. "So don't you dare try to tell me I have nothing to lose."

Xanya stood silent, desperately trying to process her friend's words and the way he said them. He'd never spoken to her like that before.

Dominic's glaring eyes stared directly into hers for a moment before he grunted and stormed back to camp.

Xanya spun to face her target again, then shook her head emphatically. *I've got to get out of here.* She turned to stare at the nearby mountains and tilted her head thoughtfully, just now noticing exactly where she was. As chance would have it, they were quite close to a place she snuck off to sometimes as a child, a place no one else knew about. *That's where I need to be.* Gruffly gathering her bow and remaining arrows, she returned to her wagon and dumped her belongings, choosing to ignore the perturbed stares of the tribe as she did so. In one smooth motion, she hoisted herself onto her horse and galloped off, leaving her people behind to go about their chores and wonder where she was going.

Chapter Sixteen

"*Now that I'm on my own, I find it impossible to escape the voice in my head. We all have one, I think. The constant nagging that everything is all our own fault, and no matter how hard we try, we'll never be good enough to fix it. Those lies are easier to drown out when you have loved ones around. Their presence is enough to prove the voice wrong. But when you're alone, you're forced to listen. The trick is not letting it tell us who we are. We have the power to break out of our heads and silence that voice for good. We just need to learn how to do it ourselves.*"

-Rafayel's personal journal

The mountains rose out of the morning mist, and storm clouds settled into the valley. Spring was finally announcing its long-awaited arrival. The snow would soon give way to a steady fall of rain. All of Enderhail would echo with the calming pitter-patter of the drops hitting every surface.

In the foggiest corner of the kingdom, Xanya walked a muddy path around a small wooded lake. She paused and took a deep breath, inhaling the earthy scent of the air. There was nowhere she would rather be than here in the impending storm.

She had walked this path many times before, always alone, always silent, always waiting. For what, she didn't know. But someday, it would happen. She started forward again, eyes slowly scanning for anything that might look different from her previous visit. Even if she didn't find it today, she needed the peaceful solitude. Others might feel suffocated by the silence, by the chill in the air. Not her.

Xanya found this secluded wood as a child, during one of the times Balthazar and Dominic were away. Any time it was close by, she stole herself away for a visit. To this day, she still thought she had never seen anything more beautiful. Nothing ever disturbed the lake's surface, not a bird, a jumping fish, or a buzzing insect. It was a shining mirror that perfectly reflected everything above and around it.

She had never told anyone about this place. Even if she wanted to, she didn't think she could reasonably come up with the words to describe it. Had anyone else stumbled upon this haven as she had? Was there some other soul who carried it in their heart as she did? If there was, she hoped to never meet that person. She wanted to feel that this place was hers alone.

A roll of thunder broke the silence but not the tranquility. The rain finally came, and Xanya looked up so the drops could caress her face. She sighed blissfully as the cool water hit her skin and removed her hair tie so she could shake out her long, ebony locks. As she slowly made her way around the path, her violet eyes fell on her favorite cluster of trees situated on the lake side of her trail.

These three trees were different from all the others in a way that she couldn't quite understand. They stood in a circle, trunks thick and covered in moss. Their branches reached out towards her like arms, twisting together in a manner much like her usually plaited hair. The roots had grown up out of the ground, making a ring of crooked and interconnected archways like a gateway to another world. Some were probably large enough for her to crawl through if she wanted. And right in the middle of the ancient giants, encircled by the natural arches, was a small hollow covered in mossy green underbrush. It looked cozy and inviting as if it would let her curl up and fall asleep in the dewy folds of the earth. It had always been tempting, but her desire to leave the landscape unsoiled had always been stronger than her desire to leave the trodden path. She always had trouble moving past this particular spot, but today, for some reason, it felt especially difficult.

As she finally turned to go, it happened.

"Xanya."

It was barely a whisper, the sound disappearing as soon as it reached her ears. She stopped dead in her tracks and whipped around. Her eyes frantically scanned the landscape for whomever had disturbed her. She slowly reached for the sword at her left hip, the tension building in her muscles.

Not another sound came, not even a rustling of the flora around her. Just the mountain silence and the thunderstorm. She furrowed her brow and turned to leave once more.

"Xanya."

There it was again, stronger this time, more urgent. Xanya whipped around, drawing her weapon as she did so. She held her breath, and once again, her eyes darted about furiously.

"Xanya." The whisper was gentler and more inviting this time.

The Huntress relaxed her weapon and slowly turned to face the twisted trees. Growing in the middle of the hollow was a warm, white light. It pulsed brighter as it repeated her name. She sheathed her weapon and looked hesitantly down at her feet and the muddy path beneath them. She'd never strayed from it. It was comfortable and familiar. It was safe. But nothing in her life had ever been about comfort or safety. It had been about sacrifice and survival. Why should this place, despite its peace and tranquility, be any different?

She had to know what was calling to her and why. The young woman closed her eyes, took a deep breath, and stepped off the path. The greenery felt soft under her boots, and she tried to step lightly so she would disturb as little as possible. As she approached her trees, the light grew bigger and brighter, beckoning her to its warmth. She lifted her arm to shield her eyes and stooped to crawl through the nearest and largest of the root arches. *"What am I doing?"* She thought. She felt a slight apprehension about what lay before her. Even in a battle where nothing was predictable, she knew what she was up against. Here, she knew nothing. Perhaps it was time to stop stalling and find out.

She crawled through the arch and was blinded by the light. Her eyes burned, and tears welled up to pour down her cheeks. She screwed her eyes shut as tightly as she could, but the glow was still visible and jarring. She wanted to turn around and go back, an unearthly fear shaking her body, but she did not move. If there was one thing life had taught her, it was that fear was not a reason to turn back. She pulled her knees to her forehead and waited, breathing deeply, willing herself to be calm.

"Xanya."

The whisper came to her ears again, kind, comforting, and...almost familiar. She slowly lifted her head and stood to take in the new surroundings. The wood was gone. She was in a broad and tall cavern, its walls made of brilliant violet crystals shining all around her. It was a breathtaking spectacle, something she could never even come up with in her dreams. The crystals were of all sizes and covered every inch of the chamber, even all the way to the ceiling. Only the black stone floor was perfectly smooth.

As she peered around the brilliance of the cavern, she saw something move in the corner of her eye. Heart pounding, she turned abruptly and found herself still alone, but something about the crystals seemed strange. Approaching the nearest wall, she looked closer at the glowing gems and gasped. What she thought was a shimmer coming from the crystals was *movement*. Each crystalline formation flickered with moving images: men and women doing their daily chores, soldiers patrolling a village, Havani people hunting for food, and...*Balthazar?* One of the larger crystals near her bore the image of her guardian's handsome face. He was shaking his head and laughing. When Xanya saw why, she choked on the lump forming in her throat.

From the other side of the gem came stomping a little Dominic, covered from head to toe in mud. Little Xanya followed, giggling so hard she could hardly stay on her feet. Dom's face was screwed up in a pouting grimace, his fists clenched. Xanya couldn't help but smile. She thoughtfully rested her fingers on the crystal.

"Stop laughing, it's not funny! She pushed me, you know!" Dominic exclaimed with indignation as he turned to Balthazar.

"I did not, you fell! I told you not to climb the fence!" Little Xanya squealed with laughter, and Balthazar's deep chuckle grew.

Taken aback by their voices, Xanya pulled her hand away. "These are all–"

"Memories, child. They are a very powerful magic."

Xanya jumped and almost screamed as the ethereal voice returned, coming from all around her. Her probing eyes searched the space, but there was still no one there.

The friendly voice tittered. *"There's no need to be so alarmed, dear. We startle just as easily as you do."*

"Who..." Xanya began hesitantly, looking around and wondering exactly where to direct her question. "What are you?"

"We are what remains of the magic of this world." The words became sad, and Xanya felt that same emotion wash over herself.

"Um, does that mean…you yourselves are the magic, or you create it?" The young Havani woman still wasn't sure who or what she was addressing. She'd been told stories of the ancient magic as a child, but they never included anything like this.

"Both, we suppose. We are magic in its purest form, created with the world as a physical force to help harness and share the power with other beings." The voice turned wistful. *"Oh, if you could have seen us a thousand years ago! We covered the kingdoms and brought everything to its full potential! There were even great mountains shining with our brilliance!"*

Xanya decided she was speaking to the crystals themselves, as ridiculous as that seemed. Nevertheless, she had to admit to her own curiosity, especially in the light of Dominic's theory about her having visions. "So what happened?"

"Evil happened. In the form of a man named Dormastis." The voice shuddered, and the crystalline walls along with it.

"I'm sorry, I've never heard of him."

"That's because we wanted it that way. We and our allies did the best we could to erase all knowledge of his existence from the world. Traces still remain, though it would be difficult and dangerous to search for them."

"Well, who was he, and what did he do?" Xanya was beginning to get impatient, though she was determined to remain polite. After all, she had no idea what kind of power she was dealing with.

"He was one of the Seven Sorcerers, the original wielders of magic. Your people worship them as gods, but they were flesh and blood, just like you. They were the most powerful and benevolent men and women who ever lived, stewards created by the cosmos to teach and protect our powers. Unfortunately, Dormastis became corrupted. His centuries-old lust for

more power overshadowed his sense of duty. He discovered a dark side of his gift, which allowed him to steal the magic belonging to others. He used this darkness to try to take it all for himself, and he very nearly succeeded."

"Who stopped him?"

"Come closer, child, and we'll show you."

Several feet in front of Xanya was a crystal growing straight out of the ground, taller than she was and as wide as the pines that grew in the forest. It now lit up like a beacon, with the same white light that had beckoned her into the ring of trees. She approached carefully, hand reaching forward, and slid her fingers up the side of the crystalline column. It was cool to the touch and impossibly smooth. The violet color shimmered and danced under her skin, and she smiled at the calm that washed over her.

Without warning, the crystal flashed with a bright golden light. Xanya felt like she was being pulled right out of the world. The tugging sensation on her mind and body was the strangest thing she'd ever experienced. Though it wasn't painful, she desperately wanted it to stop. Indiscernible images flashed through her mind, and the tugging turned to disorientation. She felt sick.

"Breathe deeply, Xanya. Using magic is something one only gets used to over time. Visiting the past is the most difficult facet of Sight to achieve."

Xanya calmed at the crystals' bidding. She breathed slowly and tried to focus on the image right in front of her. After several moments of furious blinking, she realized what she was seeing. Standing before her was a man dressed in gray robes, an ashy brown beard covering his face, and a pair of cold, dark eyes set deep in his skull.

"Dormastis."

He traversed the lands like a violent squall. People he passed cowered in fear, begging him to leave them be. A wave of his hand pushed them all to the ground as he bore down on his magic-wielding prey. A young woman of the same race as Balthazar was desperately moving her hands in a twisting motion, a violet glow sparking between them. She threw what looked like a ball of magic, and the dark man plucked it out of the air. His bony fingers pierced the glowing orb like a set of claws.

The sorcerer pulled on the orb, his hand shaking like the action was taking all his strength. He brought his other hand up to help pull the violet power into his chest, his eyes closing with satisfaction as he did so. The young woman silently screamed in agony. She looked as though the very life force was being sucked from her body. The Huntress watched in disgust as the girl faded to a dull shade of gray, even her clothes losing their color before she collapsed to the ground in a heap. With a twisted smile, Dormastis picked up the dusty scythe his victim had been using in her fields only seconds before and tucked it into his belt. He patted the blade affectionately before continuing on.

Xanya watched Dormastis rampage across all seven kingdoms of Terravalia, stealing powers and leaving dozens of grayed bodies in his wake like the very souls of his prey could not exist without their magic. As the years passed, he began to hunt more than just those who wielded the magics. Not even animals were safe from his assault. With each life he took, the sorcerer looked less and less human. His body expanded with the power until he was impossibly large. The darkening skin was pulled so tightly over his muscles that it looked like it was about to split. His already dark eyes had become blacker than a night without stars; the whites swallowed up.

When Xanya thought she couldn't take any more, the images disappeared. Looking around, she realized she was on the bank of Enderhail's largest river, facing a meadow on the opposite side of the water. It was snowing, but there was enough sunlight to cast shadows on the blanketed ground. She looked down at her feet and was startled to find them nearly transparent. It was as if she wasn't really there.

It didn't take long for her to realize she wasn't alone. Standing in the meadow was a group of Havani, all with the same violet eyes she had. They stood together, surrounded by six figures robed in white.

"The other six Sorcerers," the crystals stated. *"Ashlar, Evandris, Sabine, Tavish, Viveka, and Koromir. Dormastis waited to face them until he felt he had enough power to overtake them all at once. With them gone, he believed he could finally take the power of Sight from your ancestors, something he'd so far been unable to do. When the time came, some of your most powerful Seers agreed to stand with them. As bait."*

Xanya spoke the words out loud as the crystals breathed them in her ear. "Only the Havani race have the power of Sight." She'd never really thought about it like that. But somehow, she felt she'd known it her whole life.

The ground shook violently, and Xanya turned sharply to the left, looking for the source of the gargantuan shadow that now covered the scene. Dormastis came charging into the clearing, a roar not unlike a great beast emitting from his open mouth. He had grown a few dozen feet in height. Twisted horns protruded from the top of his head, and his feet had become monstrous paws. His teeth had turned to fangs, and saliva dripped from his protruding lower jaw, completing the terrifying picture. He was crossing the landscape at an alarming rate. Xanya turned her worried gaze back to the six beings who were protecting her people.

The Sorcerers shared a sobering look, then slowly raised their arms, palms facing their oncoming foe. The world slowed, with even the flowing river coming to a near halt. Xanya watched the six breathe together and push on the air before them. Violet vortexes began to build in the triangular shapes between their fingers.

Just as the demented Dormastis was about to overtake the crowd, the growing magic flashed white, blinding Xanya and forcing her to her knees. The ground rumbled again, and trees fell. Branches cracked as they crashed into the earth. It sounded like the very mountains were crumbling from the unnatural earthquake that shook the world.

When the chaos ceased, Xanya got to her feet and blinked away the white spots that still clouded her vision. She found her eyes filled with hot, angry tears. Dormastis was gone. The Havani were visibly dazed. And the six benevolent sorcerers lay on the ground, the breath gone from their bodies.

"No!" Xanya sobbed, and her knees went weak again. "No!" The pulling sensation began again without warning, and the mournful scene before her started to fade. She closed her eyes as the nausea overtook her body.

"It's alright now. We've come home."

Xanya opened her wet eyes and found herself back on the hard ground in the beautiful cavern. A feeling of humility, wonder, and dread filled her foggy mind. She couldn't explain why she felt such a wave of grief for people who had died so long ago. It took a few minutes for her to accurately articulate what she wanted to ask. "What did Dormastis do? What was that terrible power?"

The crystals hesitated before answering. *"We...do not know. Sadly, our own power is limited in this plane. Dormastis was the steward of Light magic, which can be fickle, but we didn't know it was capable of such malevolence."*

Xanya balked. "Shouldn't that kind of magic be everything good in the world? How did he become so evil?"

"It's not as simple as that. There is light and darkness in all of us. He wasn't always evil, we can tell you that. As we said, we don't know how it happened. Not even the other Sorcerers ever found out."

Xanya blinkced furiously in shock. Every answer the crystals gave her only created more questions. "So somehow your power fought him off?"

"It did. Through the other six Sorcerers, we were able to banish him to the Outer Realm, the very fringes of existence. Sadly, our protectors destroyed themselves in the process. We remained, however, and did our best to salvage what Dormastis had left of the world. As you can see, we are still very much alive. And as long as we're alive, magic will exist in this land."

Xanya thought she understood. As she opened her mouth to speak, the crystals interrupted her.

"You wish to inquire as to your own magical abilities?"

They can read my mind now, too? Xanya didn't know how to process anything she was hearing, let alone the memories she'd just experienced. She stood up and looked around her.

"Dormastis was ready to destroy the world as we know it. Our job was to make sure magic lived on. With the Sorcerers' help, we saved the powers of the Havani. The power that flows through your bloodline."

Xanya said nothing. Thinking you had some sort of magical ability was different from having that theory confirmed by some talking stones. The verification came with a sense of responsibility and ambivalence that made her want to squirm in her boots.

The entity around her grew reverent. *"We understand your fears, child. But magic is still part of the land itself, and your people live with the land in a way that no one else does. Therefore, your spirit can connect with us like no one else can. We will help you."*

After a few moments, Xanya was finally able to verbalize another thought. "If Dormastis wanted all this power for himself and had access to you, why didn't he just come directly to the source?"

"We no longer exist on the same plane as humans, as you might have gathered from your journey here. It is for our own safety. In order to reach us, Dormastis would have had to enter this world, which the others created and transported us to. We simply did not permit him to come here. Still, our numbers dwindle. The only way to create more magic is to use it. Sadly, not enough people can anymore. Other kinds of power and other forms of us exist in other kingdoms, of course. However, those magics are almost as rare as your own."

Xayna once again cast her gaze over the whole of the shining cavern. For the first time, she noticed not all the crystals were the same brilliant violet color. Quite a few of them were a dull, cloudy white. These did not shimmer with memories as the rest did. Compared to their amethyst kin, they looked lifeless and defeated.

"Someone is only born with the power of Sight, or any other kind of magic, when one of us sacrifices themselves to give it. Did you not wonder why we match your eyes?"

"I'm...sorry." Xanya felt genuine remorse at the thought of her abilities draining the life from one of the sentient beings that existed within these crystalline shells.

"We exist to share the power that is left. It is an honor to give our lives to fulfill our purpose. Now, we don't have much time. We must teach you how to use these powers to benefit your efforts to stop this futile conflict."

Xanya abruptly became exasperated. "Teach me? I don't even realize when it happens, I never have! When it does, it's never anything important! If I could control it, maybe I could have..." Her voice cracked as her father's dying face filled her mind.

"Seeing the future doesn't mean you can alter it. This power only shows you what might be."

"You're saying that even if I had Seen my father die, I wouldn't have been able to stop it."

"It was his time, child. We are so very sorry."

The Huntress gave a grunt of resignation. Somehow, that knowledge was a comfort to her. "Alright. So how can I make this power useful to me?"

"In time, you will be able to teach yourself more control. For now, stretch your mind. Imagine the future pulling you towards it. Feel the power within you. Reach out and See."

Xanya closed her eyes and reached into her consciousness for...she didn't know what. She tried to remember what it felt like in the past when she'd had visions, though she didn't know what they were at the time. What had been happening in those moments? She recalled the first time her tribe was attacked when she was a child. She remembered it like it was mere hours ago. They were packing to leave, and her father instructed her to help others load their wagons. The thought of her father's smiling face stung her heart. Then, she felt the memory of panic as she suddenly knew what was coming through the trees.

Her mind suddenly expanded beyond its normal human confines. Images swirled in her consciousness, and it felt as if her head was about to explode. Attempting to control the chaos, she raised her fingers to her temples, clenched her jaw, and focused on thoughts of her tribe. No, not just her tribe. She focused on Dominic. The memory of when she grabbed his dropped sword before it went through his foot. All the times they fought together, and she stopped enemies sneaking up behind him. Sparring sessions that ended in fits of laughter. The way his smile encouraged her to fight when the days got hard. With these thoughts at the forefront of her mind, the images stopped swirling and melted away until she only Saw him.

He was fighting, pushing a young boy out of the way and grabbing a shield from the soldier he'd just killed. He tossed it to Emmaline and shouted orders. He was a natural leader, taking charge to do what was best for those around him. Xanya was in awe of the man standing before her, and she wished she could tell him how proud she felt. Part of her just wanted to watch him, see what he would do. Then, he was obscured by smoke, and she realized what she was witnessing. Sometime in the near future, her family was going to be in trouble. They would need her.

Xanya was abruptly pulled from the scene, her loved ones fading into nothingness. She let out some shallow breaths and sank to the floor as she regained her bearings. The sickening feelings weren't as intense as before. That hadn't been a split-second flash before something happened. That was a proper vision. Something that was coming soon. Something she could potentially stop.

"Very good. Now you know how it's meant to feel. It can be jarring, but that discomfort will pass in time. Focus, and you will soon have more command." The ethereal voice counseled her as she got to her feet and rubbed her sore eyes. *"Remember, you may not be able to alter what you see. Don't let that keep you from fighting. This ability is meant to be a tool, not a burden."*

"I have to go," Xanya said as she cast one last glance around her, realizing that she now felt better about almost everything. "Thank you. You saved my people. You trusted us with this power. I promise I won't let it go to waste." She bowed. It felt a bit silly, but she felt compelled to exhibit the proper respect for the entity that existed in this place.

The moss-covered archway blinked open to allow her to return home. Xanya smiled. "Will I ever see you again?"

"In time, yes. Perhaps you'll also meet our brothers and sisters when the time is right. Now go, child. Do what you must. Remember what you've learned here today. Let it guide your path forward."

Chapter Seventeen

"Don't be a fool, boy. You know as well as I do that you can't run from this. Fate cannot be altered. Why try?"
-Note from Zepatra to a young King Steflan

In between mulling over the events of the past several days and practicing with her newfound power, Xanya gave herself a bit of a headache on the brief journey back to camp. Now that she'd had time to think, she felt somewhat embarrassed at taking off without explanation. Her stores of anger, grief, and disappointment had driven her away from the people who needed her most. She only hoped they would forgive her. Especially Dominic. He hadn't deserved her harsh words and attitude. It wasn't his fault her father died or that Jaheel refused to help them. He was just trying to be there for her. As he'd always been.

Xanya also wondered if perhaps Dom had been right. Maybe she gave up on Jaheel too quickly. She let her disgust and anger over his "offer" get in the way of what they needed. It wasn't like her to back away from a fight like that. *We could have stayed a little bit longer and tried to negotiate. Dom is good at that.*

She approached the camp's location and slowed her horse to a gentle trot, intending to circle around to her own wagon before alerting the others to her presence. If she could slip in quietly, maybe she'd have a chance to talk to Dom before anyone noticed.

Xanya cried out in surprise as a small band of soldiers startled her horse. The frightened beast reared, and his rider frantically gripped the saddle to stay on his back. Six armored men dodged the animal, glancing back nervously as they fled the camp.

What are they running from? Xanya calmed her mount and urged him back into a gallop, riding into the middle of the still chaotic camp. She jumped down and surveyed the minimal damage with surprise. There was no smoke and very little destroyed Havani property. Most of the bodies on the ground wore the king's armor. So, she hadn't been able to prevent her vision after all. *They drove them away, all on their own...?*

"Get started on the graves. I'm going to check in with Emmaline."

Xanya turned to face Dominic as she heard him give his orders. He wasn't wearing his armor, and his clothing was dotted with blood, but he looked relatively unharmed. *Thank The Sorcerers.* The young man he was talking to walked away, leaving Dom to give Xanya a hard stare.

She approached him hesitantly. "I see you didn't need me for this one." She offered a contrite smile and looked around. "What happened here?"

"One of the scouts met the king's men tracking us from the last camp," Dom responded gruffly. "He was able to get away and warn us before they arrived. We were ready and waiting to surprise them. They obviously haven't been met with this much resistance before, so we were able to get the upper hand quickly."

"Once again, this proves the people want to fight. You led them well." Xanya placed a hand on his shoulder. "Thank you."

Dominic stiffened but didn't shrug her hand away. He nodded in thanks and cleared his throat. "Should I bother asking where you went?"

Xanya shrugged and smiled again. "Where do I usually go?"

Dominic finally looked her in the eye with a glimmer of his usual self. "Well, I'm glad you're back from...wherever it is you usually go."

Xanya desperately wanted to take the time to talk to him and apologize, but before she could open her mouth, she felt the now-familiar tug of Sight on her mind. She held up a hand to Dom and turned sharply towards the bushes behind her, scanning for any disturbance. A slight rustling of the branches confirmed what she had Seen. She took off towards the vegetation, startling a tall figure dressed in black, who stumbled as he saw her coming and awkwardly scrambled into the woods.

Much quicker than her prey, Xanya easily got close enough to jump on his back and wrestle him to the ground. After a brief struggle, she managed to roll the man onto his back and rip the hood from his head. He grimaced as her knee dug into his shoulder. In addition to the terrified look on his face, he wore a tunic bearing the royal seal. Xanya took her dagger from her right hip and pressed it to his throat. "Didn't your mother teach you it's rude to eavesdrop?"

Only then, with the spy pathetically staring at her, did she notice his striking blue eyes. Eyes that belonged only to her people. She would have guessed him to be Havani if not for his blond hair. Puzzled, Xanya got up and slowly backed away. "You're half Havani, aren't you?" She gestured with her dagger.

The young man massaged his shoulder. "Yeah. What of it?" He got up off the ground and crossed his arms defensively.

"You'd best have an explanation worthy of such a betrayal, *daileh*." Xanya narrowed her eyes. She hoped to ingratiate herself with the spy by lapsing into her native tongue and referring to him as her kin.

The young man groaned and momentarily covered his face with his hands. "Look, I'm just doing what I have to do to survive here. That's what we're all trying to do. Please, don't tell anyone. They'll kill me if they find out."

His plea gave Xanya the confidence to lower her dagger. "I'm surprised it hasn't occurred to them already. Only we have those eyes."

"Well." the spy barely cracked a smile. "They pay well, but they're not the brightest people in the world."

The Huntress couldn't help but chuckle. She started to pace back and forth in front of him, sheathing her weapon. "How did you even end up doing this?"

"My mother was Havani," the spy answered. "When she died, my father and I left the tribe to live in the nearest village. It wasn't the same, though. Eventually, the attacks started, my father died, and I needed somewhere to go."

"Why didn't you go home when this mess started? Your tribe would have protected you."

"How?" the man asked. "I didn't even know where to start looking for them. And how many of you are left, huh? I would probably be dead by now if I had gone back to my mother's tribe. Sometimes, you just have to look out for yourself and no one else."

Xanya supposed she understood his argument, but it still didn't seem fair that he survived by becoming a traitor. She would have to let that slide for now. There was more important information to be had. "Why did you stay behind after the soldiers ran?"

"Those were my orders," the young man replied. "The king is severely lacking in information. He doesn't know how many Havani are left or where they're located. This Huntress is driving him mad. There are rumors she's planning to amass a Havani army and move against the king. She'd be severely outmatched. But honestly, I'd like to watch her try." He chuckled softly as he rubbed the back of his neck.

Xanya felt a surge of pride for her people and looked the king's man right in the eye. "What's your name?"

"Lachlan, miss. My family name is Castor."

"Well, Lachlan Castor, I need you to do me a favor." Xanya gave him a devilish grin. "Take King Steflan a message. From the Huntress herself."

Lachlan stood nervously before the king and the present members of his court. He'd traveled a great distance to convey the Huntress' message to the court. This was the first time he'd even been in the same room as His Majesty. The king's outbursts of anger were infamous amongst his forces. Lachlan had no desire to experience one firsthand.

"You actually saw her? Spoke to her?" Steflan had shot to his feet the instant the young man delivered his directive. The tension in the king's body reflected the atmosphere of the room. "She dares to challenge me?"

Lachlan finally got up the nerve to look his ruler in the eyes. "Yes, my king. If you saw her for yourself, you would understand her boldness. It's no wonder the people have been so inspired by her ferocity."

Steflan descended the stairs that led to his throne and slowly approached the spy. "You admire her for this blatant disregard of my authority?"

"No, sire," Lachlan lied hastily and returned his gaze to the ground, successfully hiding his Havani eyes from close scrutiny. "She is merely an impressive warrior. If I may be so bold, I don't believe you would disagree, sire. That is if you were to see her for yourself."

The king let out a small chuckle. He thought this boy to be a fool but also largely inconsequential. There was no need to punish the lad for simply delivering his information.

"You may go, Lachlan. Thank you." Steflan waved a hand to dismiss the spy, who hurried from the room. "Well, Oldart, you heard the lad. We've been summoned. Let us march to the appointed battlefield in two weeks' time and end this once and for all." A smattering of applause filled the room. Oldart bowed to the king before leaving, along with the rest of the assembly.

Marania stayed behind to watch as her brother-in-law moved to the large banquet table and spread out his documents. She once asked him why he didn't do his work in the library rather than have all his materials brought to the great hall. He'd merely grunted in response. However, the duchess knew the library had been Alyss' favorite room in the castle. Perhaps being in there did cause him a bit of pain.

After he requested Hemsgrid deliver some volumes from the library, Steflan sat down heavily and bit anxiously on the shaft of his pen. Paranoia, lack of sleep, and obsession had not been kind to him. His eyes were bloodshot, his body waned, and he occasionally even had a twitch. The king could feel his mind unraveling, his senses dulled by the unease that seeped into his every waking moment. He barely slept these days, checking every shadow of his chambers for intruders before he got into bed. When he did sleep, it was infiltrated by hideous dreams of betrayal that he could never remember in the morning. He ate very little for fear that someone was going to poison him. His life had become a series of glancing around corners and making hasty decisions based on very little fact or reason. Everyone in the castle saw it except, perhaps, for the king himself.

Drafting and amending laws, commander reports, and the occasional trade agreement were only the tip of the iceberg for him. Yet somehow, the mundane bits of clerical work were the only things that made him feel like himself. The continued, suspicious behaviors of some of the court hadn't escaped his eyes. He didn't know which members of his council he could trust. If he could trust any of them at all. On top of that, this Huntress character had finally decided to stop hiding in the shadows and face him directly. As much as Steflan looked forward to ending her crusade, the stories of her skills in battle made him nervous. He hadn't faced an armed conflict in quite some time. Someone younger could potentially have a physical advantage over him. *I have more important things to consider right now. Still...*

Hemsgrid came back into the room, precariously carrying half of the king's requested literature. Steflan gently grabbed his arm and looked at the older man with wide, unblinking eyes. "Have Oldart send someone to spar with me tomorrow morning, please. I need to practice."

Hemsgrid laid a comforting hand on Steflan's shoulder. "I think it would be best if you rested, sire. You've been worried to death about all this. You need to take care of yourself. We have plenty of men to fight."

Steflan took a deep breath and quelled his frustration. Hemsgrid had no right to give him orders, but the advisor had practically raised him. There was no crime in his care. "I appreciate your concern, old man, and I promise I will try to get more rest. But I need to face her myself. I will not allow my position to be subverted by this churl of a Havani."

Looking defeated, Hemsgrid bowed his head and headed back to the library to complete his errand.

Steflan turned his attention to the stack of books and empty parchment on the table. "If those people would just submit to my rule, we wouldn't be in this predicament anyway." His words were breathless like he was trying to convince himself of their validity.

Marania slowly approached and pulled out a chair next to the king. He didn't acknowledge her presence. The duchess studied Steflan's frailing form as his pen began to scribble. Given the current circumstances, she finally felt brave enough to ask a question that had been preying on her mind for many years.

"Steflan, how did you know the Havani woman who came that night? It's unlike you to be acquainted with such a person, even back then." The king had always chosen his contacts very carefully. A person like Zepatra was far beyond the fringes of his usual companions.

Steflan looked up at her, eyebrows furrowed with confusion. Marania understood his hesitation. She never called him by his first name and rarely asked a question she actually wanted the answer to.

"Do you really want to know?" The king's voice wavered.

"Yes, I do." Marania was genuinely curious and perhaps...concerned? She'd never felt that before, at least not in regards to her sister's husband. The sensation troubled her, although not as much as Steflan's knowing Zepatra did.

Steflan sighed and glanced at the returning Hemsgrid, who smiled sadly and began placing more books on the table. The king put down his sheets. "Well, alright. I suppose someone should know besides Hemsgrid and myself." He clasped his hands together. "You know I was only seventeen when I first came here. This kingdom was so strange to me. My homeland housed a Havani population as well, but they were much more...subservient to the rest of us. It unnerved me to see these people have such independence when I was so used to them obeying commands and knowing their place."

"When I stumbled upon Zepatra's shop, I was curious. I wanted to know if she was really making an honest living, as I'd heard." Steflan's eyes glazed over as his mind drifted back to that day and the fear that had gripped him. "Hemsgrid warned me not to. How I wish I had listened to him. If I had known who she was and what she meant to tell me–" he stopped abruptly, remembering where he was and who he was talking to. He was not one to show vulnerability. He never even told his late lamented wife how he truly felt about this experience. But he guessed it was too late to turn back now.

"The hag knew who I was before I even had a chance to introduce myself," he continued. "She knew where I came from. That I was preparing to marry Alyssandra. All my life, I thought the tales of the Havani Seers to be nothing but myths. Discovering those myths to be potentially true was terrifying."

Marania twiddled her fingers. "Did she tell you your future?"

"No," Steflan growled through clenched teeth, "she gave me a death sentence. My future was to be nothing but destruction and loss. She claimed I would bring it all on myself. I knew then I had been tricked, that she was merely attempting to swindle me. She must have heard the village gossip and guessed who I was, being a young stranger. I was marrying into a powerful kingdom with no debts, no shortage of resources, and no conflicts with neighboring nations. What could possibly happen that would bring about such devastation? Let alone by my own hand? The only thing I could imagine shattering the peace of Enderhail was the freedom of those Havani and their real Seers."

"If you did not believe in Zepatra's vision, why would you be so frightened of the Havani power?" Marania was perplexed. She hadn't been convinced of the woman's power either, but something must have unnerved Steflan enough to make him behave the way he did.

"Zepatra may have been a fraud, but that doesn't make the Havani powers any less real. Over the years, as I began to narrow their territories, I saw proof that some of the nomads really do possess the power of Sight. I visited their tribes, negotiated with their chiefs, and finally forced them into the farthest corners of the kingdom. My soldiers couldn't be everywhere at once, but the nomads knew the penalty if they should be caught outside their designated lands. We'd get the occasional report from scouts that they were outside their boundaries, the ungrateful fools. By the time my men arrived, there would be no trace. They must have used their powers to see them coming and fled. Yet another way they continued to mock me and undermine my authority."

"So when Zepatra came here, you felt threatened." It wasn't a question. Marania felt she knew Steflan well enough to see beneath the mask and read his moods, despite his best efforts to remain an enigma. Yet even she had no idea his tension with the Havani people ran this deep. She was never overly fond of the nomads, but her father hadn't minded them. He even asked for their leaders' input on particular issues from time to time. The current king's homeland must have been a very different place indeed.

Steflan nodded. "Over the years, Zepatra and I crossed paths a few times. Each encounter was more unpleasant than the last. She was obviously determined to torment me, though I never knew why. Before that night, the last time she tried to enter the castle was on the day of the prince's birth. Claimed she needed to speak to the queen about the child. She was denied, of course. I never told Alyss she came. You know how fond she was of those people, though heaven knows why."

Marania did know. She smiled at the memory of a little Alyss attempting to run away and live with the Havani on multiple occasions, which had made their parents laugh. The chiefs always brought her back unharmed and happy. Sometimes, she missed her sister's optimism and faith in the goodness of others.

The king choked on his next statement. "The last straw was…" He shook his head, beginning to tremble.

"I'm sorry the boy is gone, Steflan. I really am." This was still the one thing the duchess was still being sincere about. Every so often, she really did forget the part she played in the death of her sister. The child, however, never left her mind.

"If only I had some way of knowing he was still alive, I might be more forgiving. We have scoured this kingdom for ten years. He's either dead, or he's never coming back. He'll never know his birthright or who he could have become. Never know who I am or who his dear mother was." Utterly exhausted by his pretense of constant strength, Steflan let the tears flow freely, burying his gaunt face in his hands.

Marania scoffed, not bothering to hide her disdain this time. She'd had enough of this charade. "Oh, come now, Steflan, let's not pretend you had any real feelings for my sister. Your marriage was a business transaction. Nothing more."

Steflan slowly looked up. His eyes blazed beneath the tears, and his voice dripped with venom, though his response was oddly calm. "Marania, if you bothered to pay attention to anything other than yourself for a single moment, you would know how wrong you are. I may not have been in love with Alyssandra, but I cared for her deeply. She listened to me, supported me, gave me a son." He stuttered and wiped away his tears. "It may have been a business transaction," he stated, his confidence returning as he finally spoke the truth aloud. "But there's still a hole in my heart where she used to be."

Marania was flabbergasted by his response. For the first time in her life, she was at a loss for words. As she stared at him, dumbfounded, Steflan seemed to swallow his emotions and left the room in a huff, leaving his documents and books strewn about the table. The duchess stood to return to her chambers, still somewhat confused.

Hemsgrid reached for her arm. "If I may, my lady, I'm not sure you know the king quite as well as you think you do. Perhaps if you treated him more like family, you would both find someone to bring you comfort in this difficult time."

Though she knew he was thinking more of the king than of her, Marania patted the kindly old man on the shoulder and thanked him for his advice. He might have been right, but it was far too late to find out now. The walk back to her quarters was a blur. She felt she no longer had any grasp of her sister's relationship with her husband. Had she really known Alyss at all? There was a time when they knew each other better than anyone. Perhaps if she hadn't withdrawn from her sister after her marriage, Marania wouldn't have felt so compelled to begin this journey. Perhaps if she hadn't done that, she wouldn't feel so alone now.

CHAPTER EIGHTEEN

"I know you're hurt, and you don't understand. Truthfully, I don't understand either. There was no reason for Father to make the decision he did, at least not one he shared with me. Perhaps one day, we'll find out. For now, we shall continue to be sisters, just as we always have been. Nothing that happens in our lives can ever change that."

-Letter from Queen Alyssandra to her sister, the Duchess Marania

Despite the warming weather, the duchess' chambers were quite cold, and Marania felt the need to build up a fire. She supposed she should have called on Prudence, but recently, she'd found a sense of comfort in doing things herself. Perhaps she should sack the poor girl or permanently reassign her to the kitchens, where she spent most of her time now anyway. It was impractical and unfair to keep her on as a lady's maid if she wasn't being given the proper work.

Satisfied with her fire, Marania entered the small sitting room off of her main chambers and gathered her books on law. She had fully recovered from her bout of fevers and was in good spirits, especially on the heels of Steflan's public outburst. It appeared that the king's final sane moments were fast approaching. She needed to be ready to rule when the time came. At least if the Scythe would deign her to do so. It had become increasingly evident in their recent meetings that they did not view her as the queen she was intended to be. If Talis and his minions meant her to be nothing more than a figurehead, they would be in for a shock when she finally sat on the throne.

An abrupt knock came at the door, and Marania started in her chair before going to answer it. On the other side of the doorway was Lady Enid, a stern smile plastered on her face.

"Good afternoon, Lady Marania. I'm here to discuss the decision that was made in the council meeting this morning." Enid's tone didn't betray the irritating truth behind her visit.

Marania stepped aside and gestured for Enid to enter. The two had been friends long before the beginning of this mess. In fact, it had been Enid, along with Lord Kels, who first approached her about collaborating with the covert organization. The duchess had not been prepared for the strain this new arrangement would put on their relationship. Evidently, Enid thought Marania should be taking orders from her and not the other way around. Kels had displayed the same attitude, though he often left Enid to deal with Marania on her own.

Enid took a seat while Marania rang her bell for tea, echoing the weekly ritual the two of them used to share. They would simply sit and chat like old times, minus the warmth of spirited debates and pleasant conversation. They used to gossip and discuss literature. These days, they discussed soldiers and covert symposiums.

They sat in uncomfortable silence until Prudence brought the tea service and left the room. Enid took her tea with milk and two sugars while Marania drank it straight, just as they always had. The familiar clink of metal spoons in porcelain cups added an air of normalcy to the scene, at least in the absence of polite chatter.

Several more minutes passed as they sipped their tea and avoided eye contact. Enid remained outwardly calm, but Marania could feel her stomach churning. *I will not speak first. If I speak first, I'll lose control of the conversation.* As queen, she would always have to appear in control. *I might as well start practicing now.*

The duchess stifled a sigh of relief when Lady Enid finally spoke first. "The time we've all been waiting for may soon arrive. The king's decision to march against this Huntress and whatever forces she can scrape up will finally be his undoing. With our help, of course. As you know, we were all getting rather frustrated with the delay."

"If you were so unsatisfied, why didn't you just have one of your people kill him and finish it off yourselves? This could have been over years ago." Marania refused to show her anger, but her patience with these people was wearing extremely thin. They never lost an opportunity to remind her of their disappointment in the chain of events.

"Don't you think we would have already done that if it was the best course of action?" Enid got up from her seat and crossed the room to the large window to observe the activity down in the courtyard. "There's already been a mysterious death and a disappearance in this family. There must be a believable reason for his death, and he must be *seen* dying. If only to keep suspicions at bay. That's why this turn of events is so good for our cause." She turned back to Marania. "Talis will–"

"Just who *is* Talis?" Marania folded her arms and thoughtfully studied Enid's stony expression. "Despite those ridiculous masks you wear, I've been able to identify every member of your little group. Except him. He doesn't belong here in the castle, does he?"

"Whether or not he belongs here is irrelevant. I can assure you he is not someone you would wish to cross. If this plan doesn't work, someone will pay for its failure. I think we both know who that will most likely be." Enid stared Marania down as she took another sip from her cup.

"Don't you dare threaten me, Enid," Marania snapped. "Talis has made that mistake one too many times, and he will regret doing so. I don't want to add you to my growing list."

Enid looked unfazed as she returned to her seat, elegantly draping the folds of her gray dress over the arms of the chair. "I don't believe you fully understood what you were agreeing to when you joined our ranks."

"What I agreed to was your plan to give me my rightful place as queen," Marania spoke through clenched teeth. "I've done every heart-wrenching deed you've asked of me. You have no idea how that tears me apart."

"Your actions were your own," Enid said matter-of-factly. "But don't make the mistake of believing you're the one in control. If it wasn't for us, you would have no hope of ever seeing that crown on your head."

"Really? And what exactly have you and your people done to make that happen?" Marania bristled. She would no longer stand to be spoken to as a mere underling.

Enid snorted into her teacup. "Excuse me?"

"You asked me to kill my sister." Marania sat up straighter. "I did that. You told me to eliminate the heir. I did that. You told me to instigate the downfall of those Havani ingrates. I did that, too. All to prove my desire for the throne and my loyalty to you and your master. Now, what have *you* done to help *me*?"

Enid regarded her former friend thoughtfully, hiding a smirk in the corners of her mouth. "You're wondering why you need us."

"That's exactly what I'm wondering," Marania answered in a sickly sweet manner.

Enid slowly returned her cup and saucer to the table, keeping her unblinking eyes on Marania as she did so. "Tell me, how many sovereign queens has Enderhail had?"

Marania stuttered as she tried to get the words out. "Well, that depends–"

"I said," Enid interrupted, "how many?"

Chastised, the duchess slumped in her chair. "None that I'm aware of."

"Not one." Enid gave her a condescending smile. "How do you think the citizens of this kingdom will react to their first woman sovereign? Especially one who was passed over in favor of her younger sister and the man she married? That's no secret, you know."

Marania glowered and stared Enid down.

"That's what I thought. Now, how do you think they'll react to their first woman sovereign who has the power of Dormastis behind her?" Lady Enid sat back and steepled her fingers, elbows planted on the armrests. "Imagine: you're on the balcony, addressing your subjects, flanked by the cloaked figures who helped put you there. It's a scene to strike fear into the hearts of even your most dissenting critics, no?"

"No one would dare oppose me," Marania breathed, her vexation melting as the scene became clear in her mind. The Enderans reverently bowed before their new ruler and her forces. Her dream and birthright were finally realized. It would be magnificent.

Enid's voice cut through her fantasy. "Trust me, we are doing more than you know, dear. And Dormastis is very grateful for your contribution to his cause."

"Why was he banished in the first place? That is what happened to him, isn't it?" Marania had taken it upon herself to research Dormastis and the other Sorcerers, scarce as that information was in their records.

"He was very like you," Enid said. "Misunderstood and unappreciated by those who did not share his philosophies. His brothers and sisters could not recognize him for his genius, so they got him out of the way. Fortunately, they destroyed themselves in the process." She chuckled. "Now he is poised for a glorious return, and they are nothing but dust in the wind. That fact alone should tell you who was on the right side of history." The woman calmly stood to take her leave. "Be kind to those who have been kind to you, Marania. Someday, your life may depend on it. Good afternoon, *Your Majesty.*" Enid gave the duchess one last insincere smile before exiting the room.

Marania stared at the open doorway briefly before standing to close it. She laid her forehead against the sturdy wood and finally let hot, angry tears trickle down her cheeks. The rush of confidence she'd felt only minutes before had been slowed to little more than a trickle. Talis and the others claimed to be her allies, but they often felt more like adversaries, working against her rather than for her. If they were indeed the ones in control, as Enid claimed, why should she assume they would relinquish that control once the crown was hers?

The duchess stubbornly wiped her eyes and went to her desk, grabbing her legal texts as she passed them. She opened the one on top of the stack and brandished a quill, scribbling furiously in the margins and adding notes to a blank piece of parchment as she read. *Oh yes, when the time comes, the Scythe will relinquish control. I'll make them.*

Xanya and Dominic sat on the driver's seat of her wagon, listening to the bustle of the tribe, each wondering how the other was feeling.

With the preparations for Xanya's plan underway, this was the first time they'd had a chance to speak to one another. Dominic was no longer angry, but he would need a proper explanation and apology before offering forgiveness.

Xanya had memorized what she wanted to say, but at the moment, none of it sounded quite right in her head. After a few minutes of carefully considering her thoughts, she shyly opened her mouth to speak. "First of all, I would like to say I'm sorry. I had no right to act or talk to you the way I did. You didn't deserve any of it. I guess I just spent too long trying to push away my emotions, and they finally pushed back."

Dominic looked at her sadly. "You know you never have to hide those things from me, right? I know you've had so much on your mind with your father and that idiot Jaheel. You were certain Kerrigan would be the light to guide us out of this mess, and he wasn't there to fulfill those hopes." He put his arm around her shoulder and touched his forehead to her temple. "Over the past several months, you've become that light to so many people. I know you shine brightly enough to lead us out of this yourself. Don't ever let anyone tell you otherwise."

Xanya's eyes filled with tears, and her head slumped against his shoulder. "I couldn't do any of it without you. Thanks for always being here. I guess that little pep talk means you forgive me?"

Dom pulled away and cocked his head thoughtfully. "I suppose so." He finally gave her a small smile. "Next time, please just talk to me. We'll get through whatever it is together. Like we always have."

Xanya nodded and dropped her gaze back to the ground. "The second thing I need to tell you is that you were right. About my visions."

"What?" Dominic seemed genuinely surprised to hear her confirm his theory.

"Yes. I can't explain to you where I've been. If I could, you might not believe me. I wouldn't believe it myself if I hadn't seen it with my own eyes. I don't even know why exactly I was called there. But I've been given a clarity I didn't have before. Despite everything going on, it gave me the courage to move forward with our plan." She looked into his eyes again. "Thank you for opening my mind to the possibility of my powers. I wouldn't know of them now if it weren't for you."

Dom grinned and tugged on her braid. The two young warriors had found their footing once again.

Xanya smiled back and turned her attention to the tribe. "You're a natural leader, by the way."

"I'm sorry, what?" Dominic gave her a pleased, albeit confused, sidelong glance.

Xanya laughed and nudged his shoulder with her own. "I'll tell you some other time. On a more pressing note, do you think it's the right time to tell them?"

Dominic shrugged. "I don't know if there will ever be a 'right' time. I suppose now is as good a time as any. You know I think you're crazy, right?"

"Of course I do," Xanya replied with a shrug. "But Emmaline has already agreed to it, and these people have more drive than we give them credit for. If they decide to reject it, we'll do what we can on our own." She playfully ruffled his hair as she stood up in the wagon's seat, giving herself a good vantage point to address the entire company.

Dom jumped down and gave Emmaline the signal to gather the people together. They shuffled into place in front of the wagon and waited, staring at the young women above them. The small crowd was weary but eager to hear from their new chief for the first time.

Xanya found herself awash with anxiety and cleared her throat. "Well, you all know of my message to King Steflan. Now we have a decision to make together. I am your chief, but a chief's job is to guide and listen, not command. You all have the strength and the desire to fight. I've seen it." Xanya exhaled sharply and continued. "This will be an assault like never before. The choice to make a stand must be yours. If you wish to stay behind, I will accept that. However, I intend to march against the king and his army in ten days' time. Alone, if necessary."

A murmur rose from the crowd, and her gaze was met with concern and defiance. They were understandably nervous, yet she still saw that burning desire in their eyes to survive.

Xanya raised her arms to quiet her people again. "We have a few other tribes who have agreed to fight with us. I have sent scouts to inform them of what is to happen and try to recruit any other tribes they may come across. Our committed allies are small in number, but their presence will send a message that we will no longer sit by and wait to be slaughtered. The king has served as our judge, jury, and executioner for an unnamed crime for far too long. Yet he's never had the backbone to face us himself! This is our opportunity–"

She was cut off by a shout coming from the woods, drawing the tribe's attention to the trees behind them. Xanya reached for her bow and quiver as Avareck burst through the trees and into the surprised crowd, bent over and gasping for breath like he'd just run all the way back from his post. Emmaline approached and clapped him on the back as his mother brought him some water, which he guzzled at a painfully slow rate.

Xanya jumped down from the wagon and ran to Avareck in alarm. "What's wrong? Are more soldiers coming?"

Finally, the flustered scout pointed in the direction from which he came, still breathing heavily. "You've got to see. Top of Balfour Cliffs. Hurry..." He coughed as he tried to get his words out and thudded to his knees, waving absently towards his abandoned post.

Xanya looked at Dominic and bolted into the woods at a dead sprint. Balfour Cliffs were about a mile away from their current camp and a frequent scouting post for multiple tribes. The cliffs, climbable and surrounded by grassy hills on one side, were the perfect overlook of the wooded valley. Even the distant castle towers were visible on a clear day.

Sure on her feet, Xanya quickly and gracefully made her way to those cliffs, with Dominic stumbling every so often as he tried to keep up. He eventually tripped and rolled down one of the smaller hills, leaving Xanya to scale the few dozen feet of the shorter cliffside on her own. A few moments later, her hands found the grass-covered ledge, and she pulled herself to the top of the plateau that stood hundreds of feet above the valley. Pacing carefully down the slope to keep the momentum from forcing her off the opposite cliffside to her death, she finally saw what Avareck had raced to tell them. She nearly dropped to her knees, completely overwhelmed at the sight of what lay in the open meadow before her.

Several hundred Havani men and women sat on their horses, armed and stalwart, clearly prepared to fight. Their tribal flags flapped in the breeze, rudimentary weapons glinting in the sunlight that filtered through the gray clouds. She finally heard Dominic's footsteps behind her, and his hands grasped her shoulders.

"I didn't know there were so many of us left," Xanya choked out, still panting from the run. She turned to look at him, tears of unexpected joy streaming down her porcelain face. "I can't believe it."

"It's not just Havani," he replied, pointing. "Look".

The assembled tribes were surrounded by what appeared to be a host of Enderens. They mingled with the tribal members, pulling carts of weapons and armor, food and water, and medical supplies. The cries of support were loud enough to be heard even from the top of the cliffs, and the two young warriors hugged one another tightly with excitement.

"Papa, I hope you're seeing this!" Xanya shouted to the sky and pumped her fist in the air. "Oh, Dom, the only thing that would make this better would be–" She stopped abruptly as the throng below grew silent and turned to face behind them, a din of charging horses rising above the wind. Xanya gasped as *Kerrigan* rode his gray horse out of the woods, his army on his heels. He stopped his troops at the back of the gathering and started greeting and shaking hands with some of the others.

Xanya whirled to face Dominic, an expression of elation on her face that he hadn't seen in a very long time. "They came," she said breathlessly. "They came, they came, they CAME!" She squealed with sheer delight. Dominic laughed out loud as she shook his shoulders vigorously and hugged him so tightly he had to gasp for air. "Let's go, we have to get down there!" Xanya released him and turned to make her descent but paused as she came to a sudden realization.

"I can't lead an army." She gestured to the crowd below. "It's too much. You and I have a system. That's how we've always fought. A system for two people can't work for this many. The king knows how to lead an army and probably has at least twice as many soldiers." She brought her hands to her head, panic seeping into her voice as she spoke faster and faster. "The only tribesmen who have proper training and weapons are Kerrigan's. The rest won't know what to do. We're all about to march to our deaths! What are we going to do?"

"Hey." Dominic pulled his friend's hands from her head and held them at her sides, forcing her to stand as tall and straight as she could. "Listen to me. You are Xanya Fortista. The Huntress. You've done what no one else could. You inspired a rebellion against injustice. A rebellion that obviously has the support of more than just your people. We have some work ahead of us, but there's time to do it. If anyone was born to lead these people into battle, it's you." He playfully stroked his chin, "With me as second in command, of course."

Xanya smiled at him, took a few deep breaths, and looked out over her newly assembled troops. "Alright then. Let's get this army ready for a war."

Chapter Nineteen

"The battles we wage with others may seem daunting, but the battles we wage within our own souls can be most dangerous. Know your limits. Know your allies. Know you possess the strength to overcome whatever forces may torment you. I'd like to think I was responsible for that strength, but the truth is you both had it in you all along. If anything, I've only survived this long because you convinced me I could. That is your gift to this world."

-Goodbye letter from a dying Balthazar to Xanya and Dominic

The ragtag army of Havani and sympathetic Enderens rode cautiously to the appointed battlefield, a large meadow at the very base of the northern mountains. Snow still covered their highest peaks, but spring was finally alive in the valley. As always, it would be far too short, but a welcome change of scenery.

The Fortista tribes had enthusiastically joined their newfound allies in training over the past few days. Those without their own had been fitted with battle-worn royal armor left behind from raids, the king's seals ripped free of their steel backings and repurposed into smaller weapons. Under the circumstances, they were as ready as they were ever going to be.

Xanya rode at the front, leading the company along with Dominic, Emmaline, and Kerrigan. Riding behind her was Chief Grogran and several other chiefs recruited to their cause. Even Lachlin had decided to get away from the castle and was delighted to find some of his relatives still alive, willing to welcome him home. The circumstances were grim, but the feeling of community was one the Havani hadn't experienced in far too many years.

The conversation was sparse. Xanya glanced at the kindly older man riding beside her, his gentle face concealed by his graying beard. This was the man she'd expected to encounter when she and Dom had journeyed into the mountains. She and Kerrigan had a long conversation after his arrival, in which he confessed that he had been away on a supply trip when they had come to request aid. He and his wife were irate when they learned how their son had conducted himself. Apparently, this was an unfortunate pattern in his behavior, and Kerrigan finally decided he'd had enough. The disgraced Jaheel now rode in the back of the army with the least capable warriors and his mother, surrounded by his father's personal guard.

Of course, Xanya understood why he hadn't been there, but she felt compelled to ask how he hadn't known they were coming. Wouldn't they have passed one another on the mountainside or in the tunnels?

"Come now, my dear." Kerrigan had winked at her as she smiled widely. "Do you really assume that ludicrous hike is the only way in and out of our valley? How, then, would we have been able to come to your aid so quickly?"

She smiled again at the recent memory of their talk, grateful that they were here, yet nervous at the prospect of what they were about to do. They could now see their destination before them, and Xanya took a deep breath. She caught Dominic's eye on her other side to give him a reassuring smile. This could very well be their last day. They all knew it. *Be brave, Xanya. Balthazar taught you to be brave.*

They stopped on the edge of the battleground, waiting with bated breath for the king to arrive. Xanya felt obligated to say something, so she took a few strides forward and turned her horse to face her army. The army she'd fought so hard for and had doubted would ever assemble. Yet there they were, ready and willing to take her orders.

"I know this has been a long, terrifying journey," She said as loudly as she could. "I'm sure many of you never expected to end up here, about to fight for your lives. For all our lives. But I know what we can do when we come together. The people of this kingdom should not be separated by race and culture but should come together to understand and embrace our differences. If you're here, I know it's because your heart longs for a better future, one where we can all live in freedom and peace."

Dominic beamed with pride as a chorus of approval rose up from the troops, her words being passed along the ranks. Xanya saw the fire in their eyes and spoke with increasing fervor. "We shall no longer hide in the shadows and wait to die. Today, we rise up and show the king who we are!" She unsheathed her glimmering sword and raised it to the heavens, switching to the native Havani tongue. "Long live the Havani! Long live Enderhail!" Her cry was matched by all as she turned her mount and spurred him into a gallop, leading the army into the middle of the meadow. Now, they only had to wait for their adversary.

They didn't have to wait long. The rolling hills on the opposite side of the field were soon crawling with over a thousand of the king's men, His Majesty himself leading the charge.

Xanya and Dominic dismounted their horses to come face-to-face with their enemy for the first time. Nothing their imaginations had cooked up over the past several days compared to what was before them now.

Dominic whispered to her as they strode toward the approaching king and what appeared to be his captain. "We were right; we're severely outmatched. If we can broker a deal that allows us to live in peace, we won't need to engage. Let's just see what the tyrant wants."

"I can't make any promises, Dom," Xanya answered breathlessly. "He brought all this on himself. He'll need a divine explanation for his actions if he wants to get out of this without a fight."

King Steflan and Captain Oldart shared a similar conversation as they crossed the landscape to reach the young warriors.

"By the powers," Oldart exclaimed quietly. "They *are* children."

"Children who dare to defy their king. They'll get no sympathy from me." The monarch looked quite regal in his newly refitted armor, but its shine did little to hide his frail body and mind.

"I'm told by the men that she never kills in cold blood, sire. She doesn't want her own tactics to be compared with yours," Oldart said hesitantly.

"And what tactics would those be, Captain?" Steflan asked.

"Ambushing and murdering innocent victims, my king. She won't attack until we do."

Steflan scoffed. "The only thing more hollow than their claims of innocence is the illusion that they can defeat me." If he had it his way, he would instantly draw his weapon and drop this insolent girl to the ground. His position, however, required a certain decorum, even for contemptible traitors. He would restrain himself for the time being.

The four parties finally came to stand mere feet apart, sizing one another up. Steflan was visibly shocked at how small the Huntress truly was. Xanya furrowed her brows at the king's haggard appearance, noticing he was relatively young to look so worn. Unmoving, they all stared at one another wordlessly, listening to the breeze gently blowing through the grass.

It was King Steflan who finally broke the tension. "So you're this fabled Huntress who's been giving my men so much trouble. I never imagined you would be so...delicate." The king found himself thoroughly annoyed that she was such a lovely little thing. It would have been so much easier to hate her otherwise. He pulled his gray eyes away from her captivating violet ones to address the young man by her side. "Who might this *strapping*, young lad be?" His mocking query was met with a ferocious glare, and he begrudgingly admired the boy's conviction. *He betrays his people for what he feels is right. Not many men his age would make that choice, even if they were in the right.* "It's a pity you chose to fight for the wrong side, boy. You would have made a fine member of my ranks."

"I would never fight for a tyrant like you," Dominic growled. The king laughed in return.

"Enough of this childish byplay," Xanya snapped. "Let's be honest and admit that none of us want to be here. What would it take for you to stop the bloodshed and allow us to live in peace?"

King Steflan spoke through clenched teeth. "What I want, you cannot give me. The crown prince of Enderhail, my son, was taken from me by one of your wretches," He spat the words. "If you could return him to me, I would consider allowing you to live. Alas, there has been no sign of him in ten years, so we must presume him dead. That disqualifies you from my mercy."

Xanya stared at the king incredulously and shook her head. "Is this really still just about your son? Don't you think we would have produced him long ago if we had him? Nothing could be worth what you've put us through, especially not that poor boy's life. Stop pretending his tragic disappearance is the only thing that fuels your hatred for us."

Steflan glowered as he and Oldart started to back away. "Perhaps if you had taken heed of the justified orders of your king and stayed in your place, I would not have been forced to demonstrate my authority. Fight if you feel you must, but I will not lose. Not to the likes of you."

The king turned on his heel and returned to his army, with Oldart racing ahead to give orders. Xanya and Dominic charged back to their own troops, signaling Kerrigan to begin forming his companies.

Back on her horse, Xanya readied her bow and signaled to the other archers, hidden in the craggy foothills that bordered the northern side of the battlefield. They might have a slight advantage with this tactic, especially if the king underestimated their ability to strategize. She'd be shocked if he didn't.

Emmaline and Kerrigan took their place in a team at the front, as did Xanya and Dominic. The army tensed as they heard the king's trumpet sound and saw his forces begin their charge. The rebels needed to wait to advance until the precise moment.

"Are you ready?" Dominic was still worried, but their encounter with the king had fueled his anger. He was ready.

"Ready as I'll ever be." Xanya gave him a sad smile and returned her eyes to the battlefield. "See you on the other side of this." She carefully gauged the distance of the opposing army and gripped her reins furiously.

"Charge!" Her command rang out like a lion's roar. The Havani army split down the middle, riding in opposite directions to circle around Steflan's forces and prevent a retreat. Meanwhile, the Havani archers let their deadly missiles fly, doubling down on their offensive operation. Despite their much smaller numbers, Kerrigan's divide-and-conquer tactic seemed to work; the king's soldiers were obviously surprised by the Havani army's strategy and struggled to immediately respond.

Losing Dom in the crowd, Xanya fired arrows from the back of her horse as long as she could before hopping off and setting the frightened animal loose. She shouldered her bow and pulled her sword just in time to stop a royal spear from piercing her chest. Now that she knew of her powers, she was more aware of the advantage they gave her in battle. Eyes flashing with every parry, she could anticipate her foes' advances and cut them off before they even decided to move, like an involuntary sixth sense. Her concentration never faltered, moving from one enemy to the next with precision and technique.

Amid the fray, the Huntress caught a glimpse of a mounted group of people sitting on the king's side of the battlefield. They were dressed in garments far too fine for the occasion, and Xanya wondered why they were just watching. Another soldier grabbed her attention before she could dwell on it any longer.

It wasn't customary for members of the council and household to be present for combat, but Marania had desperately wanted to be present to witness Steflan's demise. Luckily, the king had been too distracted to object when she asked to be there for moral support. It was rather exciting to watch the drama of war unfold. However, the duchess had little desire to engage in that particular facet of ruling. In fact, it struck her as odd that the monarch had been so eager to engage and put himself in mortal danger. Odd and foolish. She smiled slyly to herself as she tried to pick him out in the throng. She and the Scythe would shortly have their long-awaited victory.

Amid the madness, Xanya didn't know how long the battle waged. She cut down as many soldiers as she could, tripping over bodies and slipping on the still-snowy ground as she did so. She helped a few Havani and Enderens to their feet, even pulled weapons out of wounded soldiers and handed them off to her allies. Yet everywhere she looked, she saw her forces fall. Every loss of life broke her heart, and she prayed fervently to the Sorcerers that she wouldn't find the faces of Dominic, Emmaline, or Kerrigan amongst the dead.

"You!"

Xanya whirled at the sound of the unfamiliar voice and gasped. King Steflan was just a few feet away, wild-eyed and bloodied, wearing dented armor and missing his helmet. She'd imagined this so many times, woken up in the middle of the night in sheer terror of the moment when she would finally face this tyrant, to free her people or die trying. Now that the time had come, she could somehow feel nothing but pity. The man before her was pathetic, ill-prepared, and drunk on adrenaline, hardly worthy of the fair fight she'd always wanted from him.

A manic laugh escaped from the king's lips, and Xanya's pity instantly melted into the suppressed rage that bubbled up in her veins. Her face twisted into a death glare as she white-knuckled her sword. The king raised his weapon with a mischievous grin, daring her to charge him.

Charge him, she did, with more force and speed than he clearly thought possible. Each blow sent the king reeling backward, struggling to return and block the movements of her sword. As their grudge match raged on, it became clear that the only advantage Steflan had was his size. The Huntress outmatched him in every other way.

His disgust grew, and he let go of the rules of engagement that had been drilled into him as a boy. How dare this *child* make a fool of him? In one quick motion, Steflan bashed his forehead into Xanya's, throwing her to the ground, and plunged his sword into her right shoulder. Her leather armor was no match for the direct force of his blade.

Xanya screamed out in agony, drawing the attention of every warrior around them. Maliciously twisting his weapon, Steflan finally pulled it from the girl's marred flesh and laughed again as he continued to loom over her.

Xanya blinked slowly, the ringing in her ears enhanced by her blurred vision. A flash of the assault had tugged at her mind, but his forceful blow came before she really Saw it. She simply wasn't prepared. Coming out of her daze, she finally struggled to her feet, getting her bearings back and wiping away the trickle of blood that had begun to drip down her forehead. Her right arm hung limp, the pain from her wound making it nearly impossible to grip her weapon.

Steflan stood confidently before her, prepared to accept the surrender he was confident was coming.

Instead, Xanya smiled weakly, breathing heavily and shaking her head at the bewildered king. One of Balthazar's many lessons suddenly rang out in her head: *Your body is more vulnerable than your weapon, but it can also be more versatile. Make sure you can fight with all of it.* She looked down at her bloodstained sword and gracefully transferred it from her right hand to her left, ready to fight once more. She didn't need her powers for what she was about to do.

Xanya moved like lightning. Adrenaline firing through her body, she bashed Steflan in the head with the hilt of her sword, bringing him to his knees. Expertly flipping the blade, she drove it into the flesh above his exposed hip. The king crumbled, dropping to his severely wounded side and rolling onto his back. His crimson blood dotted the remaining snow on the ground.

The fighting around them slowly ceased as word spread through the mayhem. King Steflan lay in the trampled grass, and the Huntress was the one who now stood over him, her blade poised just above his throat. The king winced in pain and glanced down at the blood flowing freely from his side. His cloudy gray eyes met the piercing violet ones that glared into his soul. In the short time since he'd first seen her, he'd come to hate those eyes. They burned with a passion that had stirred the hearts of his enemies and encouraged them to rise against him. Of all the things that could have brought him down, he never dreamed it would be a tiny young woman with a bow and a sword. Those blasted eyes mocked him. All his might had been shattered in the furious wake of the Huntress.

The king narrowed his own eyes and gave the girl a pointed sneer. He was not going to let her get away with this. "What are you going to do, Huntress? Kill me? I didn't think you were a cold-blooded murderer." Steflan knew his words were a mistake before he even finished the sentence. He gasped slightly as the girl pressed the tip of her sword into his neck.

The Huntress snarled. "You...you have spent the last ten years sending your armies after us, destroying our families, stalking us like prey, and slaughtering us like sheep. You've murdered countless innocent men, women, and children and ruined the lives of countless more! You dare imply that THIS is cold-blooded?!" Her disgust seethed into every word, her voice rising to a shout as she spoke.

Steflan shrank into the ground as far as he could, his breath coming quicker and his brows furrowed in fear. As he stared up at his foe, a sharp wave of pain emanated from the deep wound in his side, and he let out a cry.

The sound shook Xanya out of her rage, and she relaxed her weapon, leaving a pinprick of blood on the side of Sfelan's neck. As much as she hated to admit it, he was right. She didn't want to kill him. There had been far too much bloodshed already. Confident the man didn't have the strength to rise to his feet, she turned her glazed eyes to the surrounding crowd, blood loss and ten years of pain finally caving in on her. Her knees went weak.

An unwounded Dominic was finally able to push through the mob and catch her as she sank to the ground. He helped Xanya to her knees and held her tightly as she sobbed into his shoulder. All this suffering, all this death and loss, all the lives they had saved, and she couldn't summon the courage to rid the world of the despicable man responsible for it all. She had let her father die in vain. She had let her people down. How else was she supposed to finish this? How else was something like this *meant* to end?

"Steflan, dear, where are you?" An unfamiliar feminine voice suddenly sounded through the crowd.

Dom gently nudged Xanya's tear-stained face out of his shoulder and nodded towards the beautiful blonde who had forced her way through the horde. Had she been one of the mounted observers on the edge of the battlefield? She looked entirely out of place in her current surroundings, adjusting her gold and blue gown as she knelt on the bloodstained grass next to the king.

"My king, you appear to be injured. Shh. Are you alright?" Though her voice was as gentle as the coo of a dove, her passive attitude toward the king's evident pain was more than a little unsettling. She began stroking Steflan's hair, and he grunted with what sounded like...annoyance?

To their surprise, the woman looked up at Xanya and Dominic and smiled sweetly, a sparkle in her dark green eyes. She turned her attention back to King Steflan and began to hum a tune. It was slow and beautiful, sad and sweet at the same time. She broke into the lyrics, an old language that was no longer spoken. The lullaby was barely audible over the murmurs of the crowd.

Dominic tensed and released Xanya from his embrace, his eyes fixated on the feminine newcomer. He reached for the blue cloth tied around his neck, grasping it so tightly his knuckles turned white.

"Dom," Xanya entreated as her friend got to his feet. "What's the matter?"

He didn't answer but started slowly towards the odd pair on the ground, his lips silently forming the same words the woman was singing. As the young man got closer, the blonde looked up at him in surprise. Dominic managed to find his voice, and the two finished the song together before he gripped his head in agony, years of lost memories flooding back into his conscious mind.

Xanya got up and moved beside him, placing her uninjured hand on his shoulder. To her surprise, he shrugged it off and walked away from her, moving to stand directly over their enemies, fingers still pressed to his temples.

"It was you..." Dom said softly. He turned his gaze back to the woman, who looked thoroughly taken aback by his words. "I thought it was a nightmare, but..." His eyes burned with a sudden fury of recognition, and he stood taller. "You left me in the woods to die...Marania."

The woman's eyes widened in shock. She backed away, turning back to the ailing king, who had raised his head as far as he was able.

The king looked back at Marania in confusion. "What does he mean? Who is this boy?"

"I...I don't know..." she stammered feebly and tried to rise to her feet.

"No!" Dominic shouted, tears beginning to well as he pointed at her furiously. His blood boiled with a frenzy he never thought possible. "No, you won't run away from me. Not this time. I was eight! You took me, your own nephew, in the night and left me for dead. And for what?" Dom's head was still muddled, his past floating through his mind like a heavy mist. As he turned to the king, he realized who he was. What he was.

With great difficulty, Steflan sat up and stared at Dominic, his body trembling. His own eyes filled with genuine tears, his breathing shallow as he, too, came to the realization. "Zander? You're...alive...I..." He couldn't finish the sentence, disbelief overtaking him.

Xanya gasped, utterly bewildered. No, Dominic couldn't be the missing prince. But then again, she'd found him lost and confused in the woods, with no memory of who he was or where he'd come from. No one had recognized him in the villages... *Because he wasn't old enough to be presented to the people before he was taken. Royals are presented at ten! No one knew what he looked like!* Was it possible...?

Steflan looked at the paling Marania in abhorrence and clutched the hem of her dress as she desperately tried to get away. "What did you do?" He asked weakly through clenched teeth. "What..." he turned his devastated gaze back to Xanya and his long-lost son. "What have *I* done? Zepatra was right, after all." The king passed out, his head hitting the ground with a thud.

A stunned Oldart finally summoned the medics and approached Marania, who had been surrounded by guards before she could run. "Excuse me, *my lady*. If you don't mind, I'll have my men escort you back to the castle. I hope the dungeon will do." The loyal captain didn't need orders from his king to arrest someone who had apparently kidnapped a member of the royal family.

Xanya stayed several feet away from Dominic, watching him stare at the ground as the dumbfounded soldiers retreated around them. It was indeed a victory. But it felt oddly hollow and unfinished. What would happen to her people now?

Out of the corner of her eye, Xanya saw a wiry old man with a thin gray beard make his way towards them, his expression strangely both anxious and eager.

"You don't know me, and I do hate to impose," he said rather timidly. "But a particular group of the king's courtiers were watching the battle, and they appear to have scattered. I would strongly advise that you send soldiers after them."

Xanya poked her head through the tent flap and saw Dominic sitting on a cot with his head down, wringing his hands thoughtfully. She'd never seen him look so utterly defeated, and it broke her heart. He didn't look up, so she entered quietly, untying her tangled braid to let her raven hair drape over her shoulders and newly bandaged wound.

"Hey," she offered gently. "Are you alright?" Silence. *Dominic not responding to me. This brings back memories.*

She sat next to him on the cot and studied his face, looking for any signs of emotion. For the first time since they were children, she couldn't read him. She wanted answers, but for the moment, she decided to just sit and hope her presence would be comforting. It was a long while before she felt her friend stir beside her.

Dominic continued to stare at the ground, but he finally gave in to her unasked questions. "I lied to you every time I said I didn't care where I came from. Part of me always wondered. I've felt for a long time that I couldn't be something as simple as the son of a farmer or a shopkeeper. I had to be from the castle somehow, although it never occurred to me that I might be the prince." He cleared his throat uncomfortably before continuing. "How else would I know some of the things I know? Once that thought came into my mind, I couldn't get rid of it. But the castle represented the enemy, and I couldn't face the possibility that my suspicions might be true. So, I decided to figure out who I *could* be and just become him instead of dwelling on my forgotten past. You helped me do that. Despite being completely lost, you made me feel like I belonged. Now..." His voice broke, and he buried his face in his hands. Xanya reached her arm around his shoulders, pressing her forehead to his temple.

After a long pause, Dom dropped his hands and finally looked at her, letting out a sharp breath. "How can I possibly belong anywhere when I know I come from something so horrible? I'm not a prince, I'm not Havani, I'm just me and...I have no idea who that is."

Xanya waited a minute before she spoke. "Do you know why I thought we should call you Dominic? He was the greatest warrior in the history of our world. He was brave, powerful, determined, and compassionate. Willing to fight for what was right no matter the cost. You were so afraid when we first met. But you also looked so determined, and I thought taking his name would help you find your strength, your drive. Dom, you've been and done so much more. You've been by my side all these years. You've trained with me, traveled with me, fought with me. You've been my friend. No, you're not one of us." She looked into his eyes. "But you do *belong* with us. You've told me so many times where you come from doesn't matter, and you're right. All that matters is where you go from here."

She sat back and regarded him sadly. "I understand if you need to go to the castle and figure out who you are. You deserve that after all these years and everything you've been through. But if you decide not to, I'd really like you to stay here with us. With...me." She got up and turned to face him. "Whatever you decide to do, I'll always be here." She gave him a small smile and turned to leave.

Dominic grabbed her hand to stop her and stood, looking deep into her mesmerizing eyes. With only a slight hesitation, he pulled her into him and kissed her lightly. He half expected her to pull away. Instead, she drew in a breath and kissed him back. They slowly broke apart and looked at each other shyly, hearts racing.

Feeling unexpectedly self-assured, Dominic let out a sigh of contentment and exasperation. "My father is clearly unfit to rule, and my aunt will spend the rest of her days in a dungeon cell. I'm the only one who can get rid of these laws and try to undo the injustices done to the Havani people. I need to go to the castle to do that. But you're right. I do belong with you." He pulled her closer and held her tightly. "And I want you to come with me."

"I–" She trembled and pulled away slightly. "My people..."

"I know your tribes need you," he said. "But I need you too. You can help me do what needs to be done and show your people they can trust me. I have stood by you my whole life. Now, I ask that you come and stand by me. You give me the courage to fight for what's right. I love you, Xanya. That might be strange for you to hear. But it's true, and I need you with me." After ten long years, he finally mustered up the nerve to say it. He needed her to know even if she didn't feel the same for him. He looked at the ground, very aware of the fact that she was still in his arms.

"I...love you too," Xanya hesitated as she finally said it out loud, her cheeks going flush.

Dominic looked up in surprise and furrowed his brow. "What?"

"I love you too, dummy." Xanya chuckled, her nerves fading. "Did you think I didn't?"

"I...I didn't really know what you felt about me," he stammered. "We've never talked about it."

Xanya grinned and wrapped her uninjured arm around his neck. "Well, now we're talking *too* much."

Dom didn't know what else to say, so he just smiled and leaned in to kiss her again, the confusion melting away in her embrace. In a world where suddenly nothing made sense, at least they finally knew they belonged together. For now, that was enough.

Chapter Twenty

"The world is so full of impermanence. Days and years pass, people grow and change, and each season brings us closer to the end of our mortal lives. But love, the connections we make with others, is one thing that never ends. It transcends death itself. As long as we remember those we love, they will never be truly gone."

-The Legend of the Great Benevolent Warrior

"Alright then, I'll leave you to it." Xanya gave Emmaline a broad smile. When they were children, they'd been like sisters. It was nice to have that bond back. It was also a great relief knowing that she had someone to keep an eye on the tribe when she was away.

"Thank you, my chief," Emmaline said in a teasing manner and gently tucked some stray hairs back into Xanya's braid. "You know I have things under control. Now get out of here! You have a job to do."

"Right," Xanya answered and turned to leave. "I'll be back tomorrow!"

Emmaline grinned at her cousin's back and returned to her duties. She loved having her family home for good and knowing that, for the first time in a very long time, they could live in peace.

Xanya made her way through the camp and smiled at the bustling activities of the morning, offering warm greetings to all she encountered. The past few weeks had been nothing short of a whirlwind. More and more Havani were coming out of hiding, and many others were finally being released from prison. Enderens were venturing out of their villages to meet their nomadic neighbors, in some cases for the first time. Indeed, many of them were just as displeased with their king as the Havani themselves. Those who didn't yet accept them at least didn't seem to wish them any harm. Only time would tell how things would continue to progress between the two races.

The pain and suffering was still fresh, of course. It would take time for things to get back to the way they had been ten years ago. She and Dominic were doing their best to make positive changes. After days of questioning the imprisoned members, the actual plans of the Scythe of Dormastis and Duchess Marania had become public knowledge, giving the Havani the ability to travel about the kingdom more freely than they had done in years past. Kerrigan had even decided to return his tribe to the valley of Enderhail. "It's time my people remembered their heritage and stopped hiding," he'd said to her. "This land is safer for us than it has been in decades. If we are to have troubles, we now know how to protect ourselves." Even Jaheel had been happy to return to the heart of civilization despite his sour attitude toward everything else around him.

In the evenings, musical instruments that hadn't been touched in years were pulled out, repaired, and played vigorously around roaring fires while people sang and danced. It had been so long since such joy had been felt amongst the Havani people. Xanya had even been able to climb the tallest falls and finally give her father the farewell he deserved. Like his long aching soul, the Havani people were finally free.

As she reached the perimeter of the unusually large encampment, Xanya came upon Avareck's post and gave him a respectful nod. He hastily returned the gesture with a blush and turned to face the opposite direction. He'd made a few clumsy romantic advances to her after the battle and was still terribly embarrassed that she'd turned him down. She probably shouldn't have done it in front of Dominic, though, who'd been a little too pleased to witness the scout's humiliation. Unfortunately, it was too late to consider that now. She hoped they could get past it someday since she needed his considerable skills in scouting and tracking. She didn't wish to lose a good man to such a minor misstep in their relationship. "Perhaps I ought to introduce him to one of the servant girls," she mused as she reached the bottom of the hill leading to the castle. "He and Gretchen might get along well." She breathed in the scent of the warm spring breeze that blew in to caress her hair and skin. It felt strange to wear fitted black trousers and a loose white shirt instead of the stiff leather armor she'd lived in for so long. Everything about her felt comfortable, something she was still getting used to.

The great towers loomed in front of her, and the gravel crunched under her boots as she reached the crest of the hill and stepped onto the landscaped cobblestone path. Even after a month, Xanya still got nervous as she approached the castle gates. If it weren't for Oldart kindly waving her through each morning, she would insist on Dom escorting her all the way to the library himself. "Good morning, Oldart!" Xanya waved cheerfully as she passed the burly man, who'd once again left his heavy armor back in the barracks.

The captain had forgotten what it was like to have a happy young woman in the household. It certainly brightened up the place. Now that the truth was out, he felt terrible for the part he'd played in terrorizing the nomads. He was grateful for the young chief's kind heart that had forgiven so readily. "Good morning, Highness! More drafting today?"

"Yes, sir, and plenty of research. Who knew changing laws would be so complicated?" She saluted in lieu of a goodbye and made her way into the bright foyer.

After many years in such darkness, many of the castle's curtains had been torn down by order of the soon-to-be crowned new king. Sunlight poured in through the windows and gave the rooms a golden glow. The great house bustled with activity. Servants and courtiers smiled and conversed, and everyone happily greeted Xanya as she headed to the library. King Steflan and Lady Marania had been surrounded by such kind people. How could their hearts have been so hardened and cold?

Dominic sat at one of the room's several tables, books and sheets of parchment strewn across the whole surface, crossing lines out of a faded document and scribbling notes over the top of them. His chair faced the door, but he was too engrossed in his work to notice her enter the room.

Xanya marched straight to him and planted a kiss on his cheek, giving him a bit of a start. "You're at it a little early this morning, aren't you?" It was different, navigating the avenues of their new relationship. Yet nothing had ever felt so right.

Dominic smiled and kissed her hand as she hopped up to sit on the table and face him. "I know, but it turns out this is going to be a lot more complicated than we initially thought. Turns out we can't just change the law. There has to be a whole debate process with what remains of the council, a vote to ratify, and a bunch of other protections to keep us from having too much power. Hemsgrid tells me my father was getting slightly overzealous with the royal decree statute. That, combined with the Scythe's demented plans, made passing these terrible laws regarding the Havani easy."

Xanya nodded and looked around the spacious room, leaning toward Dom to speak in a hushed tone. "Are we sure we can trust Hemsgrid? I mean, he knows all about those Scythe people. He told us who most of them were, where they met, how they ended up on the council. How do we know he wasn't in on their schemes?"

"I've spoken to him about that," he reassured her. "You know Hemsgrid came here with my father when he was young. Apparently, this group was already brewing when they arrived, and they weren't terribly clever about hiding themselves from the rest of the court. At least not for long. Everyone in the castle seemed to know *something* was happening, but no one knew exactly what. Hemsgrid took it upon himself to investigate their activities and managed to find everything he needed except solid evidence. Without that, he had no case to bring against them, and their members on the council would make sure nothing ever came of his efforts."

"So he knew nothing of their intentions for your family?" Xanya asked, somewhat surprised.

Dominic shook his head. "Nor their plans to restore Dormatis to power. Wasn't that the sorcerer the crystals spoke to you about?" Xanya had finally gotten around to sharing her experience with him.

"Yes, and he was an absolute demon. I can't imagine why anyone would want to bring him back. I suppose the desire for power makes people do terrible things. Like your aunt." Xanya shuddered. She had trouble even saying the woman's name.

Dominic nodded slowly. His eyes drifted, remembering once again that cold night when Marania had taken him from his warm bed and left him in the forest. Most of his childhood memories were still faint, but that one was clear, as if it had happened only yesterday. Since regaining his memory, all he'd wanted to know was how and why this had happened.

His aunt had been less than cooperative in interrogations, barely even lifting her bloodshot eyes from the floor of her cell. The little information they did have was from a written account they'd found under a loose floorstone in the duchess's chambers. For reasons known only to her, Marania had penned every detail of both the night of her sister's death and the night nearly a year later when the old Havani woman, Zepatra, had paid a visit to the castle.

The new king shuddered himself and blinked back to reality. "Anyway, Hemsgrid may not have agreed with his methods, but he was fiercely loyal to my father. If he had known anything more, he would have told him."

"Alright." Xanya felt relieved. "He's such a dear old man. I hated to ask. I guess it's going to take a while to know exactly who we can trust. After all, these people were all close to the king in one way or another. The chamber where they had their meetings has been sealed?"

"Scrubbed, mapped, and sealed," Dominic confirmed. "We're still working on getting information out of the members we captured, and search parties are looking for those who ran."

"I still can't believe this Talis just disappeared without a trace." Xanya shook her head. "How could *none* of them know anything about him after a decade of following his orders? I'm afraid we haven't seen the last of this."

"Perhaps not," Dom agreed. "For now, we have other things to worry about. What about Zepatra? Have you been able to find out anything about her?

"Not really." Xanya pinched the bridge of her nose in exasperation. "I've asked around, and no one knew her, though plenty of people have heard *of* her. Evidently, the last time she was seen was the night she came to the castle. The guards in the courtyard saw her leave, but there was no sign of her past the gates. The woman is a ghost."

"Was she really a Seer?"

Xanya shrugged in response. "No one can tell me that either. If Marania's description of her blue eyes is accurate, I doubt it. I suppose she could have been mistaken. But there was definitely something strange about her, whether she had the power of Sight or not." Xanya hesitated, reluctant to even ask her next question. "There's still one thing I don't understand. After Marania...killed your mother, couldn't she have just married your father and ruled that way? This plan of hers seems a bit convoluted."

Dominic shook his head. "That's not how it works here. According to the kingdom charter, when the king's daughter gets married, the inheritance is transferred to her husband. The only way for a woman to have sole rule is for all other heirs to perish."

Xanya's frown deepened. "This whole business is just so messy! I don't see how she thought it was the simplest way to get what she wanted. And we still don't know why they targeted my people too."

Dom gave her a sad smile. He couldn't pretend to comprehend his aunt's behaviors, let alone know how to explain them to someone else. Clearly, she was not a stable woman. "She believed her birthright was stolen from her. Evil people took advantage of her desire for power and convinced her that was the only way to get it. Somehow, your people just got caught in the crossfire." He paused, and stared at Xanya thoughtfully. "We need to figure out a way to ensure the queen has just as much political power as the king. If I'm away, or if, Sorcerers forbid, something happens to me, I want you to be the one in charge. We can't risk something like this happening again."

"We'll change the laws as much as we need to. Then all we can do is hope it's enough. But we can't guarantee a perfect system." Xanya laughed nervously. "I think we've seen firsthand what people do when they get desperate."

"What a messed up family, huh? I really rolled a winner in the gene pool." Dominic rolled his eyes.

"Oh, I don't know." Xanya leaned forward and gently brushed the hair away from his face. "You turned out alright."

"I was raised by a good man alongside my best friend. I hate to think what I might have become if the king had raised me." Dom glanced up at the imposing portrait of King Steflan and shook his head. He was strongly considering having it removed from the room. Truthfully, he didn't know how to feel about the man. His disgust and anger were mixed with morbid curiosity. Who was Steflan, really? Was he really nothing more than an evil tyrant or merely a man whose grief had driven him to the edge of madness? He doubted he'd ever know for sure.

"Well, based on the stories I've heard, I'd say you're more like her," Xanya said.

Dominic followed her gaze to the portrait of his mother on the opposite wall. He took in her light-hearted smile, her eyes, and her wavy brown hair, exactly like his own. "There's definitely a resemblance," he agreed.

"No, I mean you're *like* her," Xanya persisted. "Kind, compassionate, willing to fight for what you believe. People adored her. You're probably more like her than you'll ever know."

Dominic smiled up at the painting, and then his eyes widened. "Oh!" He stood up from the table and crossed the room to one of the smaller shelves. He came back holding an ornately carved wooden box. "Hemsgrid found this tucked away in the king's quarters." He opened the box and lifted out a beautifully jeweled silver tiara, very different from the golden monstrosity that had sat on the head of King Steflan. Dominic's grin widened. "This was my mother's."

Xanya hopped off the table and peered at the glittering object in his hands. It was made of delicate silver leaves wrapped around one another and connected by twisting vines. Small white diamonds graced the headband, and a dark green emerald sat at the tip of each leaf. "It's the same one from her portrait. It's even more beautiful in person."

Blushing over his giddy smile, Dominic placed it on her head and directed her to the full-length mirror in one corner. Xanya slowly stepped closer and studied her reflection. She'd never had anything even remotely like this on her person. Somehow, it felt like it had always belonged to her. She reached up and untied the leather cord from her braid, letting her long raven hair hang loosely down her back.

Dominic moved behind her and placed his hands on her shoulders. "Hemsgrid said she would be happy to know her crown will be sitting on a Havani head."

Xanya also blushed as she stared at the two of them together in the mirror. Her eyes lit up, and she carefully drew her sword with her uninjured left hand.

"It matches the hilt," she said as she set the tip gently to the floor and struck a regal pose. The weapon did indeed resemble the silver headpiece, with the emerald adorning the hilt and the filigree that graced the bottom few inches of the blade. If Xanya didn't know otherwise, she would assume they'd been made by the same hands.

"Balthazar never did find out anything about this weapon, did he?" Dominic took it from her and carefully slid it back into its scabbard as she turned to face him.

"No, he couldn't even find a description of it. But you know, I've decided that it's somehow connected to the crystals. I mean, they essentially said I was a part of them. Maybe they knew I would need help." Xanya's eyes grew misty as she remembered the sparkling cavern, though she still didn't quite understand what had happened. "That may not be the case, but for now, it's good enough for me."

"Well, if that's true, I need to thank them for creating my beautiful warrior queen." Dom stroked her hair and leaned in to smother her laughter with a kiss as Hemsgrid swept into the room.

"Excuse me, Highnesses, I–" He stopped when he saw Xanya's jewelry, and a huge smile spread across the old man's face. "It suits you, Miss Xanya. The late queen would be very pleased, very pleased indeed."

Xanya offered a clumsy curtsy as thanks. The maid, Prudence, had been trying to teach her, but the Havani woman was not entirely convinced her legs were meant to bend that way.

The advisor's smile slowly faded as he addressed his new master. "Your father is about to leave. He would like to speak with you. Shall I tell him you are unavailable?"

Dominic's face hardened. "No, I'll speak to him." He squeezed Xanya's hand and left the room. She paused briefly, then strode after him, carefully placing the tiara back in the box as she passed the table.

Hemsgrid stopped her at the door with a gentle touch on the arm. He glanced up at the painting of the queen and smiled again at the new lady of the house. "She would be so incredibly proud. Of both of you."

Xanya gave the old man a tight hug, then continued into the hallway and down the stairs to the open back door of the infirmary, where the king had been recovering.

King Steflan had never looked worse. Though the physicians had miraculously stitched up his wound and confirmed he would live, the man would never walk again. Discovering the truth behind Marania's scheme with the Scythe had been the last straw for his health. His mind and body finally succumbed to the pernicious illness that had been growing for years, fueled by stress and paranoia. He lay weakly on a gurney held by two pages, who would deposit him in the waiting carriage. Steflan was being sent to one of the smaller country houses on the other side of the kingdom, with only a few servants, a nurse, and a handful of guards to look after him. His life would be comfortable but isolated, left to spend the rest of his days contemplating the mistakes that had ruined his existence.

Dominic stared down at the pathetic creature who had created him. As much as he wanted to hate him, all he could feel was pity. "You wished to speak with me?"

The ailing man coughed and wheezed, taking a breath that sounded painful. He turned his head to his son and spoke weakly. "Zander..."

"That is not my name." Dominic tried to keep his voice even, though he momentarily prickled with anger.

"My son..." Steflan coughed again. "I wish I could express my regret for the wrongdoings I have perpetrated. I was weak with hatred, and evil people used that weakness to manipulate me. Their sinful deeds do not excuse my own. I was so blind to the fact that I could have stopped all this before it even began. It will haunt me for the rest of my days." He looked straight into Dominic's eyes. "Promise me you will be a better king than I was."

"I promise." Dominic wanted nothing more than to keep that promise, not for his father, but for his people and his future wife and children.

Steflan shifted his gaze warily to Xanya, who had crept up behind Dom. "You...take better care of him than I could have. I daresay you've already done just that."

Xanya nodded as the pages carried the gurney across the courtyard. "Safe travels," she offered softly and waved. The boys placed the former king into the flatbed of the carriage and hopped on the back to ensure his safety during the journey.

"That was kind of you," Dominic remarked as the driver urged the horses onward. "You didn't need to do that."

Xanya leaned back into Dom's chest as he wrapped his arms around her. They watched the carriage make its way down the path towards the village.

"Yes, I did."

EPILOGUE
A FEW MONTHS LATER

"Do dreams have meanings? I cannot say for certain. However, I would be lying if I didn't say there have been times when I have awakened and felt that my dreams were trying to tell me something urgent. And I wish to the Sorcerers that I had listened."

-Notes from an ancient Havani philosopher

Darkness swirled around her like a living mist. She couldn't see anything but the flecks of black dust and ash that grazed her face. "Hello?" Her cry was met with a heavy, suffocating silence.

Out of the silence came a low, menacing growl. The growl slowly became a gravelly voice, deep and dripping with evil. She couldn't hear what it was saying. As she strained her ears, it grew just loud enough for her to make out the threatening words.

"I'm coming for you."

Xanya shot up from her drenched pillow. Her breath came in short bursts, cold sweat dripping down her forehead. The blankets were mangled and twisted like they'd just lost a brutal battle. The night was still black as coal, and no moonlight shone through the open window. The glow of the dying embers in the fireplace was the only thing to assure her of her surroundings.

Dominic sat up next to her, his eyes bleary, his hair a frizzy mess. "What's wrong, love?" he mumbled.

The Huntress turned to her husband, her violet eyes wide with dread. "Something is coming from beyond the mountains."

PRONUNCIATION GUIDE

Enderhail- Ender-HALE

Havani- Huh-VAHN-ee

Xanya- ZAHN-yuh

Rafayel- Raf-AYE-el

Marania- Mar-ON-yuh

Emmaline- Emma-LEEN

Avareck- av-UH-wreck

Enid- EE-nid

Dormastis- Door-MASS-tiss

Sabine- SUH-bean

Mytra- MITT-ruh

Havani Language Translation:

-Lochrage- a derogatory form of the word for a non-Havani person, not often used and considered extremely rude

-Daileh- Havani term for kinsmen, used amongst the tribes to refer to others of their race

Acknowledgements

I have never been on a journey quite like this, and I couldn't have gotten through it without the support of so many friends and family.

To my husband, Russell, thank you for helping me through all my insecurities, tears, and impulsive decisions. And also for talking me down from quitting so many times. I'm lucky to have such a patient and loving man in my life!

Thank you to everyone who generously read through this book's early versions and give me much-needed feedback. Whether through comments, lunches out, or even just gaps between our computers on a slow workday, you really stepped up! You taught me so much about taking constructive criticism the right way and using it to improve my work. You're all the best!

To my writing groups, who are there for me every single day, thank you for sharing your knowledge and talent! I can only hope to one day help out another newbie author half as much as you've all helped me.

Kristina, my developmental editor, you were invaluable in showing me the weaknesses in my work but also the strengths! The amount of confidence you gave me to keep going was unexpected and more appreciated than you can possibly know.

Kaitlund Zupanic, thank you for sharing your incredible artistry in designing my amazing cover. I knew you could put the best face on this project, and you exceeded my wildest expectations! I can't wait to see what you'll do next!

There is one more specific person without whom this book wouldn't exist at all. Annalise, you're one of the best friends I've ever had and the only person who knows as much about this fictional world as I do. Thanks for being my cheerleader through this whole thing. I truly couldn't have done it without you!

And lastly, to you, the readers, thank you for taking a chance on this little story! I hope you enjoyed it, and I can't wait to share the next chapter of Xanya's story.